A Mother's
DISGRACE

IMPRINT
lives

A Mother's
DISGRACE

ROBERT DESSAIX

Angus&Robertson
An imprint of HarperCollins*Publishers*

An Angus & Robertson Publication

Angus&Robertson, an imprint of
HarperCollins*Publishers*
25 Ryde Road, Pymble, Sydney, NSW 2073, Australia
31 View Road, Glenfield, Auckland 10, New Zealand

First published in Australia in 1994
Reprinted in 1994

National Library of Australia
Cataloguing-in-Publication data:

Dessaix, Robert, 1944 – .
    A mother's disgrace.
    ISBN 0 207 17934 4.
    1. Dessaix, Robert, 1944 - . — Biography.
    2. Authors. Australian — 20th century — Biography.
    I. Title.
A828.309

Typeset by Midland Typesetters, Maryborough, Victoria.
Printed in Australia by Griffin Paperbacks, Adelaide

9 8 7 6 5 4 3 2
97 96 95 94

Acknowledgments

I would like to thank Yvonne, my mother, for her frankness and generosity in sharing her thoughts and experiences with me; Peter Timms, for his support and confidence during the writing of this book; and the many other friends who encouraged me over a number of years to write my stories down. I would also like to thank the Literature Board of the Australia Council whose grant made the writing possible.

For Yvonne

CONTENTS

'I'm telling you stories. Trust me.'
Jeanette Winterson, *The Passion*

CHAPTER ONE

Groppi's

One warm April evening in 1984, in a pleasant suburb of Cairo called Zamalek, three exquisite young men tried to kill me. A dance with knives and a pricking at the throat that began with a coffee at Groppi's and ended, not with a severed wind-pipe, but, oddly enough, with my finding a voice.

If you've ever been to Cairo, you'll know Groppi's. Everyone at some time or other drops in to Groppi's for tea and perhaps a *palmier* or an almond slice dusted with icing-sugar. Inside Groppi's, with its cool, high ceilings and its art deco furnishings, Cairo in all its raucous seediness and squalid grandeur suddenly seems pleasantly far away. I felt safe there.

I'd wandered in alone in the late afternoon, past a knot of chiacking youths, to contemplate the evening. It seemed a shame to waste it, the next day being my last in Egypt, but then again the walk back through the dusk to the hotel might prove adventure enough. So I just sat amongst the dim mirrors and the warm smells of pastry and coffee and let the evening distil.

Suddenly there was a scraping of chairs and two sleek young Cairenes sat down at my table, lean-faced and grinning.

1

A Mother's Disgrace

Had I been followed in? There was an awkward question or
two (the usual kind: 'Where are you from? Where is your
wife?') as I drank my tea, and a taut kind of pleasure as
well.

Then the oddest thing happened. Up bowled the waiter,
sharp as a knife, and said: 'I can't serve you if you talk to these
two men. You'll have to leave.' Nonplussed, embarrassed, I felt
my *savoir faire* desert me instantly. I needed a pithy retort, in
simple English. None came. Mohammed and Farouk slid in
behind the table on my right. Face had been saved all
round, it seemed.

In time, across the gap between our tables, an edgy conversation started up again. Lots of grinning, lots of subtext, but
could I read it? Mohammed, slender to the point of gauntness,
nervous and fine-boned, did most of the talking (he was
married, one small child, off to Athens on the boat from
Alexandria tomorrow), while Farouk, somehow softer, less
the chisel, smiled and nodded with just a hint of surliness, the
merest pout. A photograph came out (no sign of the
waiter) ... 'My wife and child'. I seem to recall they were in
Frankfurt—somewhere far away at any rate, somewhere
prosperous, waiting. We were all waiting. The ceiling fans
filled in the silences.

Eventually they left, still grinning, ambling gracefully
through the doors. They'd thrown the dice and thrown
well. I didn't even know I was playing.

About ten minutes later I, too, strolled outside into the
muggy heat to head back through the traffic and the touts to

my hotel across the river. The street was full of yellow light and people lounging, strolling, shouting, murmuring in smoky clusters. It was a street of men. Not far in front of me I caught sight of two men pushing an ancient cream Mercedes up the street, one behind and one half in the driver's seat. Mohammed and Farouk. The Mercedes bucked and coughed and stopped. They grinned at me. Mohammed called me over. 'Come for a drive,' he said, straightening up and rasping something at Farouk. 'You help us push. We'll go for a drive.' Why not? The Mercedes bucked into life and off we lurched. Cairo was now deep mauve.

What pleasure is there to compare with driving fast but aimlessly on a balmy night across a new city? I once careered around Paris at night on the back of a motorbike, a gold helmet on my head, swooping across squares and bridges, past eerily soft-lit classical façades, along the Seine, up crooked, cobbled laneways, going nowhere, except in my head. Thomas his name was. I'd only known him for half an hour.

To be frank, you can't really swoop through central Cairo. Every artery is clogged, especially around Tahrir Square. But after a while we seemed to be at least puttering steadily through a more suburban landscape, with streets of apartment houses, mosques and churches forking off around us at crazy angles. And then we were gliding in and out of these streets quite quickly. I was deliciously lost. At one point we drew up at the gates of some vast, dark pleasure garden, thudding with loud music. Mohammed said it was a disco, but the gate-keeper wouldn't let us in. We backed out into the stream of traffic again. I didn't care.

Now, apart from the occasional adjective, I'm telling you the version of what happened I was later to tell Sergeant Mustafa. Over sixteen hours in his tea-coloured office I told Sergeant Mustafa what happened so many times, and from so many angles, that I have come to believe this version is the true one. I don't think he ever quite believed it. But what Sergeant Mustafa was most interested in was what happened next.

We drew up at the door of a fairly featureless middle-class Cairo apartment block: five or six sand-coloured storeys, with balconies jutting out here and there, a cavernous entrance hall, no one much about. We could have been somewhere in behind the beach at Bondi or St Kilda. Mohammed leapt out and called up to an apartment on the first floor. Lounging next to me on the back seat Farouk seemed to be giggling about something. A head appeared over the edge of the balcony above. There was a brief exchange.

'That's Hassim. He says to come up and meet his mother.' Mohammed looked pleased. Husky sounds from Farouk.

Hassim's mother? Why not? Lots of smiling, probably, and sticky things to eat and mint tea. More questions about where my wife was. I'd met Arab mothers before in long, cushion-lined rooms off courtyards in Morocco. God alone knows what they'd thought or in what time-honoured story, if any, they'd seen me as a character.

We clattered up the stairs and met Hassim in the doorway, a little plumper than the other two, a little glossier and a little fairer. Inside, the apartment was large and cluttered with objects—carpets and hookas, brass jugs and paintings—but no mother. That was curious but difficult to know how to construe. I didn't try.

I no longer remember what we talked about. Perhaps Sergeant Mustafa has a list of subjects written down in some yellowing file. I probably toyed with a mineral water while the boys drank Algerian wine (I'm not much fun in these situations) but I do remember saying no to hashish. (Sergeant Mustafa became very alert at this point in my tale, but not because he admired my virtue.)

At some point I got up and went to the bathroom, a small, windowless room in the middle of the apartment. A minute later someone banged loudly on the door. Too loudly. Almost trying to break it down. I opened it. Farouk flung it wide and stalked in . The soft side to him had vanished. As I told Sergeant Mustafa:

[The suspect known as] Farouk fondled me in an ambiguous way, grasped the silver chain around my neck and tore it off. (A bolt of fear.) *He then seized my wrist and roughly removed my wrist-watch.* (The fear begins to surge.) *I protested. He then produced a knife and pressed it into my neck. Then [the suspect known as] Mohammed entered the room and locked the door behind him. He pushed Farouk to one side and began to hit me. He ordered me to take my clothes off. As I did so, Farouk began*

5

dancing around me, speaking excitedly in Arabic and jabbing at me with his knife. My bowels opened involuntarily. I was terrified. (All I can think is: 'What a waste. What a waste. What a waste.')

Then [the suspect known as] Hassim began banging on the door and calling out. After some minutes, when I was naked except for my underpants, Mohammed opened the door, argued with Hassim and then pushed me out of the bathroom into the adjoining room. I was thrown onto a divan. All three men gathered in the room (Farouk still dancing madly with his knife) *and began arguing in Arabic.* (I thought I was going to die. I felt utterly naked, bereft even of self. The room was filling with the stench of my faeces.)

I don't know what people usually think when they're about to die suddenly and stupidly. I know, for instance, that in my case my life did not flash before my eyes. Nor, strangely, did I pray (as I might well have) or feel any rage. My strongest feeling, as I've mentioned, was of waste. Here I was, a forty-year-old man, healthy, educated, with every prospect of an interesting, fulfilling life ahead of him, throwing that life away on a whim. And the flimsiest, the most banal of whims. I also remember feeling deeply humiliated. Who'd have thought, who'd ever have thought, that I'd end up naked and shit-smeared with my throat cut on a Cairo rubbish dump? Broadly speaking, a very Protestant response, despite the lack of prayer.

My other thought was much more down-to-earth but in its

own way no less Protestant: P. was waiting for me in Rome, no doubt wandering at that very moment around the streets near the Pantheon looking for somewhere cheap but still Roman to eat. The adventure of our lives, starting the day after tomorrow. With a walk, perhaps, in the morning sun through the gardens of the Villa Borghese up on the hill behind the hotel. I would never arrive. Total abandonment. The big full stop.

Then the Arabic turned into English. I started to feel real again. Farouk had stopped snaking around with his knife, Mohammed had stood up. Hassim stayed strangely hunched on his chair by the lamp. 'Get dressed now,' Mohammed said. 'Quickly.' A flutter of hope, the feeling that somehow I might have lurched into a different storyline. My trousers were damp with dribbly shit, even my socks seemed soiled, but I wasn't about to quibble. Then, as I later told Sergeant Mustafa:

The three men stood at the door to the apartment, opened it and told me to leave. They pushed me out, abusing me as I went. They then came out onto the landing to watch me walk down the stairs. As I left the building, I turned around to see the number of the building in the street. It was written on a metal plate in Arabic, which I could not read. A middle-aged man in European dress was passing the house. I asked him in English if he would tell me the number of the house. He did. It was number seven. The three men were watching and started running down the stairs towards us. I ran off up the street.

Foolishly, as it turned out, straight up the middle of the street. Past a restaurant called Le Don Quichotte (its bright yellow neon began blinking in my brain), still no one about except the middle-aged man now a hundred metres behind me, past a Coptic church awash with lights—some kind of celebration, a noisy crowd of people milling around in front—and then the street darkened. I kept running, just away, into blackness. Suddenly I heard a car coming up very fast behind me. I squeezed in between two cars parked on my left. The Mercedes sliced past me, bruising the knuckles on my right hand, then screeched to a halt. I went rigid with terror. Then ran. Across the road, up a side street, around a corner, wild with terror. Le Don Quichotte, Le Don Quichotte, Le Don Quichotte. Headlights behind me. The Mercedes again. It accelerated fast. I leapt out of its path and veered back the way I'd come. Had it stopped? Would they chase me on their young men's legs?

I then came to a night-club, I think by the river, with a taxi-stand in front of it. I took a taxi to my hotel (ashamed of my stink). *The clerk at the desk paid for the taxi. I then went to my room, Sergeant Mustafa, locked my door securely and stayed there until this morning.*

I was in the grip of a new fear now: that my snarling dandies, my elegant thugs, would come to my room in the night and throw me from my twenty-second-floor balcony with its expensive view of the pyramids. I stood at the door half the night, my eye glued to the peep-hole, expecting to see them loom bulbously into view in the misshapen corridor outside.

Drawing the beige curtains across the view of the pyramids, I sat down at the desk by the beige lamp and started to rewrite the story so far. *(For you, Sergeant Mustafa, a version for your files.)* Leaping up from time to time to hold my breath and stare through the fish-eye in the door, I retold myself the evening through the dead hours until dawn over and over again, until I got it right. On Sheraton bond. I didn't feel crushed by what had happened, you see. In fact, if anything, suspended there writing at some nameless hour in the silence high above Cairo, anonymous, disconnected, some part of me was now spiralling upwards. On words, then phrases, sentences and whole stories. Who I was—had been, would be—suddenly seemed so fluid, the self so evanescent, protean. A word, a name, and by some magic a precarious self would crystallise briefly in the void and float there, many-faceted and glinting. And then dissolve. It was a dangerous moment and I soared on it.

Yet surely, I said to myself, I had a real history. Or, to put it another way, I had lived a real life—an almost inexcusably unremarkable one, some might say. For a start, I'd had a not unhappy childhood as childhoods go. I'm not at all convinced now that happy childhoods are a good thing, I think they can lead to a kind of moral paralysis, a sort of smug Swissness of the spirit, but once you've had one there's nothing much you can do about it. Adopted as a baby towards the end of the Second World War, I grew up in lower middle-class comfort, if that's the right word, on Sydney's lower North Shore. We only had an ice-chest when everyone else had a refrigerator, we had no car, no telephone and no television set when all our neighbours had them, but we were not impoverished. It was an unremarkable house we lived in, wedged between the primness of a lawn-edged street out the front and the wildness of a bush-filled gully behind. (In secret ways those two boundaries—the primly mown buffalo verge on the street and the bush at the back, dense with night sounds and animal possibilities—still function as boundaries to my sense of who I am.) My unremarkable parents were middle-aged and irritated with one another and loved me (I now know) like a beautiful thing that might break, but it was they who in fact broke and died, one mad. Abandoned (as I saw it) first by my natural mother and now by Jean and Tom Jones I tried to make a life by being married—it was by now the early 1970s—and by excelling at my chosen craft of teaching others in minute detail the largely superfluous things from Russian culture I'd mastered myself. My wife and I lived for a time in all sorts of far-off places—Moscow, Helsinki, Paris—criss-crossing the world from Kashmir to Peru and from Java to Lapland on study trips of one kind or another.

Abandoned yet again (as I saw it), this time rather abruptly by my wife, I moved to Sydney, thought I'd seize life by both hands and put an ad in the personal columns. In 1982 I met P., took up with him or he with me, and two years later off we flew to Europe for a grand tour, he straight to Italy and I via Egypt. And so I came to Cairo, to Groppi's and to my spiralling moment on the twenty-second floor of the Sheraton Hotel. And although it grew out of a sense of nothingness, of being stripped bare of any self, of being brutally silenced, untongued, reduced to animality, it was also a luminous moment in its way. Perhaps in George Steiner's terms it was even quite a Modernist moment, the point at which the covenant between my lived life and the stories I'd told myself about it broke.

There was something not inappropriate about having these thoughts in Cairo within sight of the pyramids. My natural mother's name—and my own since Jean and Tom had died—was Dessaix, a name to conjure with, a name that promised stories, not like Jones. Now, in the annals of the Dessaix clan, Egypt has always had an important place. In very different circumstances from mine, Napoleon's general, Louis-Charles-Antoine Desaix (one 's') de Veygoux landed just outside Alexandria in 1798 on his way to conquer Upper Egypt, of which he was to prove, according to my *Nouveau Petit Larousse*, an 'administrateur équitable'. In the accompanying postage-stamp-sized portrait he looks more foppish than fair-minded, I must say, but it's a small entry between Demosthenes and Descartes and a lot of meaning had obviously to be packed into that one bland word 'équitable'. It was Louis Desaix de Veygoux my natural mother Yvonne had in mind, I'm sure, when she said to me on the day we first met after forty-five years: 'Remember you come from Very

Good Stock.' And she rapped on the table we were sitting at three times. Did I really? And in what ways did it matter? And what precisely was stock? *De très bonne souche* you say in French, especially of dogs, *souche* giving rise to thoughts of sturdy trunks with deep roots in rich soil.

Yet when I was brought home by Jean and Tom Jones, Aunty Moat across the road said I looked as if I might be Aboriginal. In 1944 that was a slur you had to pay for. I might be cross-eyed and swarthy, but I had actually been certified a Good Adoption. Every year for seventeen years, at Christmas and on my birthday, Aunty Moat would atone for her offensive observation by giving me a book about Art and a cake of expensive soap. Unwittingly, she did me a great service, because without her books I'd never have known what names like Cézanne, Picasso, Braque and Mondrian meant. Certainly, no one else would ever have mentioned them.

Aunty Moat lived in a Spanish-style house, with white walls and tiles on the floor, and was artistic. She was a neighbour, not an aunt, but in those days, as you'll no doubt remember, neighbours formed clans, sang songs around each other's pianos, gave each other eggs from their chooks, helped each other build garages, quarrelled and cried on each other's shoulders. Unless, of course, you were Catholic, which was considered extremely poor taste, like farting in a lift. Only old Mrs Edwards was Catholic in our part of the street and she did the decent thing and kept to herself.

In point of fact, my father Tom himself had been brought

up in a large Roman Catholic family as one of thirteen brothers and sisters (and half-brothers and step-sisters). The women in the family, as Jean pointed out, seemed prone to using nail-polish, even on their toes, and to drinking beer and smoking and knowing the names of racehorses. Fortunately, the family seemed to do most of its proliferating in South Australia and, although my father throughout his long life retained that large-family, perhaps even Catholic, geniality, conviviality and tolerance of others' foibles, he had drifted away from the religion long before I was born, probably when he was a merchant seaman before the First World War. If the local parish priest ever dared show his face on a pastoral call, Tom started up the Victa. Tom was living proof that Catholicism is not like polio. Given a lively imagination, a childhood infection can be permanently cured. If he'd been forced to cast a vote it would probably have gone to something rather more theosophical than traditionally Christian. We used to have arguments about reincarnation over the washing-up.

It was there at the sink that I first heard my father's theory about another Egyptian connection. Well before I could write (I suppose I must have been about two or three) I used to concoct long columns of what my father, with Madam Blavatsky's encouragement, no doubt, was sure were embryonic Egyptian hieroglyphs. Some Pharaonic earlier life or, more prosaically, a rogue Egyptian gene (he knew about the General) might have been casting its shadow. You don't have to believe it, of course, to find it adds a dimension to living.

My mother Jean was of quite a different cast: of Scottish stock, rather Calvinist by temperament, although, as a nurse (and she went back to work when I was still a very small child) she had a practical streak when it came to the human body. I caused a furore in our part of the street when I was about four by telling all the children I could the amazing news about where babies came from. The MacFarlanes two doors up didn't speak to us for three months. And when I was briefly and quite undramatically molested on the way home from school one afternoon, Jean lost no time in explaining to me in some detail what 'men like that' did with little boys. I was warned to keep a weather eye out for men wearing socks and sandals, especially if they were sitting on park benches. So in my mind the socks-and-sandals brigade joined women who wore nail-polish on their toes as socially undesirable and the long alliance Tom Keneally has alluded to between virtue and pride was forged. We never got around to men who wore nail-polish on their toes.

But back to Cairo. On this last day in Cairo I had actually meant to visit the pyramids, scene of Louis-Charles-Antoine's heroic victory over the Mamelukes, barely glimpsed to the west in a shimmer of heat and sand from my hotel balcony. That glimpse was all I was ever to get because from the moment I appeared at the Tourist Police at nine o'clock that morning, script learnt, in pursuit of justice (scion, you see, as I liked to think, of the equitable Louis), Sergeant Mustafa, mustachio'd and alarmingly swarthy, took me over. We sat in his shabby, yellowish office from nine until one. He drank tea copiously, served by a grey-clad peon of some kind, who slithered in and out with his wet tray of glasses, but none was offered to me. I went over my script from start to finish and finish to start many times. We started in the middle and went backwards, we started near the end and inched forwards. We hopped about in it, zigzagged, turned circles, dived, but I was word-perfect.

Something deeply interested Sergeant Mustafa about the case. It wasn't, needless to say, my stolen watch or silver chain. What was it? He flirted with the possibility of a sexual subtext to my story, but there was nothing of that in my script. He seemed bemused. There is, we both were thinking, more to this than meets the eye. But isn't there always? Eventually, we went outside into the smoky glare, got into his car and chugged two miles to Zamalek. It took forever in that nightmarish, car-choked, boiling city and Sergeant Mustafa seemed disinclined to chat. We were heading, as it turned out, for Le Don Quichotte. We found it, parked and ambled up the empty street to number seven. There were the heavy glass doors, the cavernous entrance hall, the stairs. Sergeant Mustafa went up to the first floor landing (I was watching from the street) and knocked on the door. No answer. He then knocked on the neighbour's door and this time had more luck. A quick exchange and Sergeant Mustafa came down the stairs, two at a time now, reinvigorated, on the scent, and off we drove towards the bazaar.

The man who owned the flat (Hassim's father) was known to Sergeant Mustafa, he told me, and we just might be onto something. Now, this wasn't in my script. I wasn't sure I wanted to be onto anything, not sure any hashish-dealing on the part of Hassim's father, for instance, was necessary to my tale. By this time on this Cairo afternoon I was hungry and thirsty and starting to fray around the edges. On the other hand, the hero of my tale was standing up quite well, I thought, and Sergeant Mustafa must not know the difference. Somewhere in the bazaar near the walls of the University we found the shop where Hassim's father, in air-conditioned comfort, sat in a glass box and traded in expensive bric-à-brac—brass jugs and reticules and necklaces—and, perhaps, we thought now, in one or two other things as well. But what a charming man he proved to be: tall, grey-haired, with cultivated manners, quite the gentleman. I watched them from outside through the glass. And he watched me.

Then back we chugged to the office in the late afternoon and settled down to wait for something. What? As it turned out, several numbing hours later, for Hassim. By now Sergeant Mustafa had an assistant, somewhat thinner, sharper, intent on nibbling away at my well-established tale. At me, in fact. Hour after dry hour the three of us tossed back and forth the details of the night before. He said, I said, they said, they drove, I went ... And then at about nine o'clock in the evening Hassim was brought into our stuffy room, now brown and shadowy with just one bare electric light-bulb burning.

Hassim was in a state of abject terror, he was wild-eyed with

16

it, quaking, weeping. I nodded and he was led away again. I felt numb. What would they do to him? Would they put his head in a bag full of chilli-powder and roll and kick him on the floor? Or would daddy be encouraged to suggest another approach?

Sergeant Mustafa and his assistant now left the room, leaving me alone in its brownish fug for the first time in over twelve hours. The door was open. Was I being invited to leave? Not just yet. Hassim's father came in now, smoothly grey and speaking faultless English. How very unfortunate the whole thing had been. Surely I would agree that his son had played only the most minor of roles. Would I like some tea? I would? With sugar? No? The thing was that poor Hassim, although of course he'd been foolish to let those brigands in, would now find his whole career at Cairo University blocked, his life, so to speak, in ruins. Would it not be better for all concerned to let the matter drop? He realised I was out of pocket over the whole thing and happily would let me have ... let's see, he happened to have right here with him now some English pounds, quite a few, as a matter of fact ... not to put too fine a point on it, some hundreds. Might not they make good my loss and ...

No. I got quite stony. Whatever game he or they or we were playing (and I'd long since lost track of the rules), he'd mis-played his hand: my virtue (my pride) was now doubly offended. And anyway, if I was not mistaken, it was the father, not the son, who was on Mustafa's hook. He'd be better off slipping the good sergeant three hundred portraits of the Queen, not me. Games with three players are always treacherous. He left in silence—not, I fervently hoped, to wait for me outside with some more violent offer.

Sergeant Mustafa and his assistant drifted back in. It was now close to midnight. I was nearly speechless with fatigue. I said I wanted to go. (Why hadn't I opted out earlier, I began to wonder? I wasn't guilty of anything, I was a free man. Why didn't I just get up, thank them for their trouble, if not for their hospitality, and go?) Ah, well, you see, they hoped at any moment to bring Mohammed and Farouk to the station. They were on their track. It was important, in order to snare the father, to get the three boys talking. And to get them talking they needed me. But I had a plane to catch to Rome, I said, in just a few hours' time—I could hardly remember at what time—four-thirty, five. I really had to go.

Wouldn't I stay another day and help them catch their fish? Suddenly the room began to smell evil. I wanted to get out. All right, they said, you can go. But first you must sign a statement. Wait while it's prepared. We waited shiftily. The assistant decided on one last nibble. Lean-faced like Mohammed, quite young, quite wiry beside his heftier boss, he fixed me with his cat-and-mouse-game gaze and said: 'Are you quite sure there was no ... sexual proposition to you at any point?' 'None,' I said, faithful to the end to what I'd thought was the agreed script. After a while the statement arrived. It was in Arabic. God knows what it said or who had written it. Yet another version of the night's events, presumably. I signed it and left. It was one o'clock in the morning. I'd been there sixteen hours. A few hours later I took off for Rome and that walk with P. in the Villa Borghese. I told him the story, of course, although in yet another version from the one I'd told Sergeant Mustafa, from the signed Arabic statement, and from Hassim's and from the version Mohammed and Farouk were perhaps at that very moment having beaten out of them. But they were now on their own, locked into a storyline I could not rewrite for them. Turning round to look back over the roofs of Rome on that warm April morning in the gardens on the hill, I was already in another life.

As it happens, just for the record, in March 1800 Louis Desaix also left Egypt for Italy, but with unhappier consequences. Mid-afternoon on 14 June at Marengo in Piedmont he finally came galloping up to Napoleon, who had been faring badly all day against the Austrians. Cannons were thundering and the air was filled with smoke and the stench of death. 'Alors, mon chef,' he's supposed to have said, glancing at his pocket-watch, 'il n'est que trois heures, il reste encore le temps de l'emporter.' ('It's only three o'clock, we still have time to win.') Nearby, at Vigna Santa, at the head of the 9th light infantry brigade, he was shot through the heart with a single bullet and fell dead from his golden-tassled horse. An elegant enough death, if a trifle sudden. In fact the French did go on to win the day, but Napoleon was anxious to take credit for the victory, despite his supposed affection for the young general, so Desaix's contribution has been covered in silence for the last two hundred years—a statue here, a nondescript street named after him there. A recent historian has even claimed Napoleon had his general assassinated. Whatever the truth of that accusation, he died the same day as the treacherous Kléber was killed back in Cairo, the same Kléber he had fought with in Egypt, yet Kléber has an avenue and a metro station named after him in Paris. Not that these official silences and twistings of the facts are of much real consequence to me now. Eventually a grosser fabrication came to light.

And speaking of false leads, red herrings and outright lies, four years later in Sydney I had another pivotal experience which grew out of that moment in Cairo. It grew out of it because in my spiralling upwards that night I realised that in all the stories I'd told myself about my life up to then I'd always circled around the question of my mother. (And father, too, in a vaguer way, but there were no real stories about him, he always seemed to me to play a bit part.) It was partly out of pride (I felt so self-made), partly out of fear of what or who I might find and partly because I didn't know how to start. After Cairo I wanted to fill in this shaft of silence running up through the centre of my life, at least with words. I didn't think much beyond a story. But in April 1988 something simply happened.

CHAPTER TWO

Motherlands

Peg was in William Street in Sydney's seedy inner east looking for my office. William Street, if you don't know it, is a grand avenue gone hideously wrong, a hideous cock-up of a boulevard, very Sydney, sweeping down from the birthday-cake Town Hall into the jumble of Woolloomooloo and then up again to the gigantic neon Coca Cola sign on the hill at Kings Cross. Scattered amongst the hamburger joints, futon shops and car sales rooms down in the trough at that time were the offices of the ABC. Peg was late and confused about which building my office was in. Westpac? Westfield? That red brick tower further up the hill?

In the cool of Westfield Towers she scanned the list of tenants. Dalwood, Driscoll, no Dessaix. She stopped a middle-aged woman on her way out to lunch. Did she know a Robert Dessaix in this building? Well, you ask that kind of question when you're running late and it's warm and muggy and you have to *do* something quickly. No, said the woman (Peg barely focussing on her now), she didn't, but it was odd that Peg should ask because she had been a Dessaix (or so Peg reported)—Yvonne, as a matter of fact, her name was. Anyway, Yvonne knew where the studios were, if that was any help, because she worked for the ABC too, and a few minutes later Peg came bustling into the studio where I was waiting, a bit on edge now, and as she settled herself in behind the microphone to tape her review for my program she told me half over her shoulder what had happened just a few yards down the road. About this Yvonne Dessaix.

I was thunderstruck. While one part of me taped Peg's review of a Mexican novel, another part of me slid backwards into silence to crouch there, speechless and bewildered, pondering what to do. Just a few yards from where I was sitting, in Westfield Towers, a middle-aged woman called Yvonne Dessaix was returning from lunch. That was my mother's name. She was my mother's age. How many middle-aged Yvonne Dessaixs could there be in Sydney? It was 1.35. By 1.40 I could have met my mother. Everything could change, for her and for me, everything could be transformed five minutes from now. If I chose. But as the other part of me chatted with Peg and the operator, suggesting a retake here and a longer pause there, scribbling notes on the script and answering the phone, the quieter, crouching part was sliding further back into silence. She might not have ever told anyone, she might want to forget, she might not approve of me, she might be happy with four children and have loud, crowded Christmases every year with so many presents under the tree she lost count, she might cling to me crazily and go mad at the end like Jean. I was fine, I'd made a life, I was me, without her, let her go, just pass quietly by, let it rest ... The taping was finished now, we moved out into the stairwell and my two selves edged together again. 'Bye, Peg, thanks a lot, see you later.' As she clattered off down the stairs, I turned back towards the studio, restored to myself and feeling strong.

But before I even got back to the studio door, I wheeled around, flew down the stairs, across the street and down the hill, through the Westfield foyer, and into the lift. Four, three, two, one floor above me was my mother. Here ten yards, ten seconds from where I stood, was my mother. We would collide. I'd willed it. Excuse me, where's Yvonne's office? Around the corner? Second door? The door was open. There she sat. It was not my mother.

How do you know such things? Are there pheromones or something? Before me at her desk sat a smallish woman, not quite petite, perhaps, but open-faced, immediately friendly, lively eyes looking up at me ... but not my mother. A delicate moment, wouldn't you say? And a profoundly sobering one.

I can't now quite remember what we said to each other. Something about how odd it was we'd never bumped into each other before—of course, her name was not Dessaix, but still my program had been going to air for several years, the name is so unusual, you might have thought ... And how did I fit in? Yvonne was not uninterested in family history. Exactly what I'd feared. 'Oh, I come from Canberra,' I said (only a half untruth). I'd always found that stumped them. And my father? 'Dead,' I said, 'no trace. Interesting to have a longer chat some day.'

'And are you Catholic or Protestant?' she said. What was this new minefield? I took a step. 'Well, Protestant,' I said. 'Oh, that explains it,' said Yvonne and looked relieved. 'Ever since grandfather Andrew lapsed, the Catholics and the Protestants haven't spoken. That explains it.' Good.

'And do you by any chance know of any other Yvonne in the family—about your age?' I asked. Risky but worth it. Here Yvonne got interested. She knew of an Edna, a Sophie (was it?), a Maude ... but no, no Yvonne, sorry ... Well, maybe it did ring a small bell—something about a dress-shop—but no, not really ... why did I want to know? 'I seem to remember my parents being friendly with an Yvonne just after the War,' I lied.

And so we smiled and said how very interesting, how nice to have met, some other time perhaps, we really ought to ... She was to retire in just a few months, I should ring ... And down I went in the lift and back to work, still stunned, but differently. I felt put in my place. In time I even forgot this not-my-mother's married name.

In the end, though, Peg's chance meeting with Yvonne that day forged the link I lacked between my mother and myself. It took some time, some thought, and some courage, on both our parts, and the story didn't end as either of us might have thought it would with tears, unbounded joy, completeness, pumpkins turning into golden coaches. But then, it hasn't ended.

I've often thought about the element of chance in this, of course—how could you not? Chance is dangerous because it

24

subverts the most rational of personal philosophies. But I couldn't help thinking later, when the false Yvonne was replaced by the true, if Peg had stopped another woman, if she'd been held up at the traffic lights and got there ten seconds later, if I'd not asked Peg but someone else to review that Mexican novel, if I hadn't met Peg in Mexico City, if I hadn't got that job at the ABC, if, if, if … Pointless, I know, and no doubt quite wrong-headed. Life simply isn't linear like that. It's much more curved.

❖ ❖ ❖

Let me describe to you a city I know well, but you could not be expected to. The old town, where some of the zigzagging streets are still cobbled and the castle keep called Mokkó still stands intact and grey-black on the highest point, is on a promontory at the mouth of a small but swiftly flowing river. If we walk north from the keep, away from the sea (a choppy strait, with the mountains on the offshore island clearly visible to the south in good weather), we come to a more ordered, European part of the city—almost like Helsinki, really, with gracious Palladian buildings (mostly ochre and cream, but some duck-egg blue) enclosing thinly planted squares and lining well-planned streets. There are a few cafés and restaurants dotted about the streets here but if it were lunchtime and we wanted a more crowded, bohemian atmosphere we might head more east towards the escarpment above the river. This is the part of the city that was 'outside the walls' in an earlier century, so the streets are narrower and more crooked and the buildings quainter and pokier. There's the odd glimpse across the river below to pines and sand-dunes on the other bank. If you wanted something more up-to-date—shopping malls, glass and chrome delis, that sort of thing—you'd have to go northwest from the centre, out into the suburbs stretching between the sea and the mountains just a few kilometres inland. Down on the sea on the other side of the promontory from the river is a pleasant little bay—in fact, that's what it's called in the local language, The Little Bay—with a promenade and some expensive private houses with lush gardens on the hill behind. It's quite a high hill—well, it curves round to form the promontory—so if you're down on the promenade at the water's edge you can't see the mountains hemming in the city from the north or the magnificent monastery, almost a Potala, soaring up brown and white and sheer above the foothills. Idyllic, really, although the winters can be severe.

This city does exist, but not quite in the same way as, say, Vancouver or Wellington. I don't wish to sound mystical, but it's existed for me since I was a small boy of about six, pottering around in the backyard where the bush came up through the chook-yard to the edge of the back lawn. It was there in that backyard I started to imagine my own Pure Land. It wasn't just a fantasy or a game I played there with myself; it was and still is a parallel world.

Not long ago I stood looking at a Tibetan painting of Shambhala in the Royal Academy in Piccadilly. Shambhala is a word which changed over the years in English to become Shangri-la, which sounds more evocative to our ears, I suppose, but also more vulgar. At the centre of this painting is a round, white city, Shambhala, the Pure Land. To the eye it's Lhasa-like, clustered on a mountain like a flock of goats. There are no people in this round city, just houses and pavilions and a maze of alleys. Around this city, this Pure Land where perfection and non-being are somehow one, lies a ring of mountains, then a ring-shaped sea, then another ring of mountains and another sea—seven rings of mountains in all and seven seas. I stood immersed in this Tibetan painting for a very long time. It meshed quite miraculously with the pure lands I'd inhabited in my mind most of my life—like my secret island it's the embodiment of myth and at the same time 'real', lying just off the coast of India—and it also meshed with the sense I have of a more circular inner geometry.

I say that because, as a Westerner, I've been brought up to see life as linear, sequential and consequential, as heroic or tragic, modelled ideally, perhaps, on Jesus of Nazareth's or less loftily on any adventurer's. Yet deep down I know that a life can be pictured, construed, made sense of in terms of a completely different geometry altogether. With nothing at its core. I'm no mystic—there's a kind of Gallic rationalism in me so deep-seated I can't meditate for more than five minutes without tumbling into analysis and measurement and the prisonhouse of language—but this Tibetan painting seemed to me to map my life in a way more conventionally dramatic geometries did not.

Like the painting in the Royal Academy, my Shambhala too had streets and houses, rivers, lakes and mountain ranges and was an island. Already at six I could have drawn you a street map of the main city (severely rectilinear) and pinpointed it for you in my school atlas: it was (and is) just south of the Aleutians in the North Pacific. For tuppence in those days you could take home books from the musty one-roomed shop at the edge of the local shopping-centre we called the Library. I often borrowed books about the Arctic, especially Iceland and Greenland. There weren't many, so I took home the ones they had many times and I think the map of Iceland impressed itself on my consciousness early on and helped to shape my own Land. I hesitate to tell you what I call it—it's not that it's sacred or a secret, it's just that I want to keep it pure. And I fear your scorn.

Perhaps it's a case for psychiatric intervention, but over the four decades since I first drew a map for myself of the Righteous City—all right, call it K.—with its righteous rectangles, its parks and squares and public ponds, my Pure Land has not clouded over and disappeared from view as it ought to have done, but has grown denser and more economically and politically complex, and my map of the city has spread into a map of the island. And across the island snake railway lines (I used to know the timetables) and roads both paved and unpaved, there are airports, hospitals, castles, police academies, monasteries, prisons, cafés, theatres, bridges, mines, hotels, even benches in particularly sunny spots on certain promenades. I can tell you the rates at the health farm in the mountains near the Blue Lake or take you on a tour of the Buddhist monastery on a clifftop in the south. I can recommend certain cakes in a café in a town called V. (oddly enough, a mainly Russian Orthodox town and an important site of Orthodox pilgrimage) and run through the family history of the eighteenth-century rulers of the district of B. I live there, after all. Even as I write this, I realise I'm being careful not to tell you a single untruth.

A lively imagination in thrall to a single obsession, you're thinking to yourself, *The Magic Faraway Tree* gone pathological. Possibly so, but not a total waste of time. It took about twenty years for me to realise that through the matrix of this imagined Motherland, unaware of what I was doing, I was working out and articulating to myself all sorts of religious, philosophical, sexual, psychological and other problems. While studying one religion, for example, in my everyday life, I was actually elaborating and entertaining other religious philosophies which flourished in my land (more gnostic in tenor, although I didn't know the word). While eating meat I could debate radical vegetarianism as provincial government policy on an offshore island. As my distaste for Eastern European socialism strengthened, I could write articles defending it in my head for the Party daily newspaper in the north of my Land, where a Communist government had been in power since 1947. A fortified border cut the island (and my psyche) in two. It came down several years before the Germans demolished theirs, at about the time I settled down with P.

But it gets madder. When I was about eleven I started reading up on artificial languages—Esperanto, of course, but also Volapük, Pirro's Universal-Sprache, Interlingua and other concoctions. I was starting to learn Latin and Russian, already spoke a little French, and for £2/1/6 I bought myself a copy of Frederick Bodmer's *Loom of Language: a Guide to Foreign Languages for the Home Student*. So while other little boys were playing cricket in the street after school or going to Scouts or torturing small animals, I was comparing Greek script with the Cypriotic syllabary, musing on sound changes in medieval French and learning quite a lot about the differences between Swedish and Danish, not to mention Dutch, from the fascinating word lists in the Language Museum at the back of the book. All this must have been having some effect on the sort of teenager I was becoming.

One effect, apart from a complete lack of interest in cricket or indeed in playing any kinds of games with little boys, even cards, was the immediate need I felt to create a Pure Language for my Pure Land. I would set up my own loom and weave my own language. Now, many children make up private languages, I know—sisters talk with brothers in secret codes, only children compile private vocabularies, prepubescent fraternities have their ritualistic gobbledygook and so on. But starting from the age of about eleven I began to do something much more ambitious and, I suppose, eccentric: I began to construct an Indo-European language of enormous grammatical and morphological complexity, with a history going back to pre-Roman times in Asia Minor, sound shifts, three scripts (one syllabic, thanks to the Cypriots), two main dialects and several regional variations on those dialects. If I'm alone and in a compulsively Pure-Landish mood, I'll chat to myself in this language (the dialect depends on the persona I'm entering) and certainly all my dogs have heard a lot of it. As far as I know, no one else has ever heard or read a word of it. (Well, you've actually read one word, *mokkó* (n., neut. sing. nom.): 'a small keep' (from the root *mok-* 'to close off').

This is madness sprouting madness, you must be thinking. I suppose it is in a way, but my rational self seems powerless to stop it. It just proliferates in my head like a vine. Part of me lives there and has done for over forty years. Although I do remember making resolutions on significant dates (my twenty-first birthday, for example, my thirtieth birthday, a New Year's Eve or two) to give it all up like masturbation, to put it away like some childish thing, it's not something I can just swear off.

English is filtered through it all the time. I make myself translate almost everything I hear—phrases from conversations, the titles of books and films, news items, advertisements. Obsessively, I force conjunctions to occur between language systems. Meaning only occurs in conjunctions, after all— words and things, words and words, words and memories (the universe and God, for that matter). If something just hangs in a vacuum (like a godless universe) it has no *meaning* as such at all. So I hear a phrase like 'right and wrong', for example, and think to myself: now, how would I say that in my language? And immediately I'm aware that 'right and wrong' are just English words with a history. They've been applied to different things at different times in different social contexts, of course, and whatever translation I choose can't be expected to come with the same baggage. The history of my Land is, after all, very different from England's, as are its mores, its value systems and its social structures. And so, as I try out this word and that (bearing in mind, let's say, that both the English 'wrong' and the French 'tort' have to do with twisting), groping for a way to express this phrase in my own tongue, I become intensely aware of how relative and personal concepts like right and wrong are, how socially determined, and how imprisoning knowing just one language can be. And over the years that's been true of many key words in my psychic development—obvious ones like 'good', 'evil', 'God' and 'love', over which I've battled with myself for decades, but also more peripheral ones like 'home', 'friend', 'intelligence'—yes, and even 'mad'. This kind of awareness changes absolutely everything. It was having to say to myself in my own language 'I love him', 'he loves her', 'I love rhubarb', 'I love Mozart' and 'God loves me' that first made me ponder what love means. These are lengths mad Billy Liar did not go to with his fantasies about the Republic of Ambrosia. But Billy Liar, unless I'm mistaken, was trying to escape from a dreary middle-class post-war England. I don't think I was trying to escape from anything.

In some ways all I was trying to do by spending part of my

time in a parallel world was to belong somewhere, to give myself a history I had some control over. I'd known ever since I could know anything that I didn't come from where I was. Wisely or unwisely, Jean and Tom had told me before memories begin that my mother and father had not been able to keep me and that they, Jean and Tom, had wanted to have me very much because they couldn't have their own children. So on the one hand I seemed to have landed on my feet while on the other, from a very early age, I was confronted with the fact that there are times when people must abandon those they love. As I grew older I seem to remember the story changed a little: my father had died in an air-crash and so my mother had married someone else. (Strangely close to the truth, as it turned out, but not something Jean and Tom should have known.) I was also told my mother's maiden name and that it was French. Once Jean even cut a photograph out of the social pages of the *Daily Telegraph* showing a group of smiling middle-class women one of whom was a Dessaix. She came from a nearby Sydney suburb. I remember feeling intrigued but not deeply moved.

On hot afternoons on the back verandah Tom, now sixty-odd, would sit learning French from phrase books and grammars in order to speak to me in French—and not just *passez-moi le beurre, s'il vous plaît*, either. Given that he'd left school at about twelve in 1901, the son of pub-owners in Port Augusta, this was no mean achievement. And it went further: he took out a subscription to *Le Courrier australien* and joined a society for French-speakers, something rather more demotic than the Alliance française—sailors from French ships used to appear at the get-togethers (*les amicales,* they were called), songs were sung and long rambling stories were told, just the sort of thing Tom revelled in. And when Jean went back to work we had a cleaning-lady from Noumea I used to talk to in French—a small-boned, waspish woman who pursed her lips so tightly I could hardly understand a thing she said.

None of this was affectation, it was generosity of spirit, it was an offering. Tom was a man with a big, soft heart and a kind of Irish love of words and the games you can play with them. *Satu, dua, tiga, empat, lima* ... I see him again now, in his old Hawaiian shirt and shorts, sitting on the back verandah with the races switched off, teaching me to count to ten in Malay, which he'd picked up in the merchant navy forty years before, and then in Pushtu, which he'd learned from the Afghan camel-drivers passing through Port Augusta in the 1890s. He wasn't averse to telling my mother and me over dinner what 'thank you very much' was in Cantonese, either, or in Russian (he'd been to Vladivostok before the Revolution), a habit which seemed to nettle Jean. She took delight in mispronouncing his French phrases—*oh, mercy buckets*, she'd say, or *Quel horror! It's pleuting!* We weren't fazed.

It *was* moving to think that I had been abandoned by a beautiful French mother ('pretty and petite' was how Jean put it—I scarcely wondered how she knew) and by my brave and handsome father the pilot. He always remained nameless and mysterious—all I knew about him was that the almoner at the hospital where I was born had thought him 'very good-looking'. What was moving to me as a child was the story, not the facts. The idea of being reunited with my mother, strange as this may seem, did not much interest me. At least, not in real life. Of course, I used to fantasise that my father was King of Bessarabia and that my kingdom would be restored to me, that out there somewhere, perhaps on the next tram I caught or standing in line at the fish shop, were brothers and sisters who looked exactly like me (no one else seemed to, after all) and who would reclaim me right there on the tram or in the fish shop. And when for some years in the late 'fifties I worked in a large city bookshop during the Christmas school holidays, I used to dream that one day a woman would come up to me with a book and say: 'Charge it, please, to Yvonne Dessaix.' What on earth would I say? I was moved by the scene in my head, and went over and over it, but I don't know that I really wanted it to happen in real life, right there in Paperback Fiction.

Much more interesting than meeting my mother by then, in my mid-teens, during stolen moments in Foreign Languages, was encountering Jean-Paul Sartre in French. And André Gide soon followed (*Si le grain ne meurt, L'immoraliste* and others). This gave rise to a shadowy Impure Land in my head. French and France were suddenly cloaked in deviance and desire, eroticised, not just by sexuality, but more powerfully, perhaps, by being simply so deeply *knowing*. Over there they *knew*. Over there they knew things and said things (in

French) no one ever seemed to know or say where I came from. I had led a rather sheltered adolescence.

I actually bless the sheltering. I elected to be sheltered. One afternoon, on the back verandah, I sat watching Jean washing the sheets in the copper, stirring them with a big smooth stick. I was nine. I got up (I remember this vividly), walked over to the laundry door and said to her: 'I don't believe in God.' Jean kept stirring and asked me what I meant. I was troubled mainly by the little coloured pictures we were given to stick in a book each week at the Presbyterian Sunday School in Longueville, where I'd been christened. I had been under the impression all these years, as I collected these pictures of Jesus feeding the five thousand and teaching under date-palms, and listened to stories about Jesus and the Flying Doctor and the awfulness of Communism, that Jesus had been a good man, a teacher, a bringer of good news about God and what happened when you died. Then, as I swung on the front gate one evening under the jacaranda arguing with some Catholic cousins, it had been brought home to me that some people really believed that this Jesus of Nazareth was God. I was outraged. I'd never heard any-thing so absurd in my life. It was like being told that trigonometry had turned itself into a first-century Jew—or music or loving-kindness. But when I checked with my Presbyterians and found out that they, too, thought that the Nazarene was actually God, I decided to put my foot down. They tried to palm me off with a story someone had come up with several hundred years after the Jewish *nabi* had died about a Trinity. I'd have sooner believed in Father Christmas. I'd been hoodwinked.

Jean kept stirring the sheets. Although not a church-goer, she was spiritually inquisitive, a seeker less after Truth, perhaps, than balm and comfort. So, although I was only nine, she considered what I was saying seriously and answered me in a way that changed the entire course of my life. 'There's a church, you know, that doesn't teach that Jesus was God. It teaches that God is Mind—mind is what God is—and that Jesus came to teach us this. Mrs Fogg goes. You should go with Mrs Fogg.' Jean knew about this teaching from her days as a nurse in a children's hospital. You're not supposed to say this sort of thing in educated society, but she'd seen it work miracles.

The very next Sunday morning I was up at the bus-stop in good time for the bus to Chatswood. A few minutes later Mrs Fogg, a gentle, grey-haired woman who lived up the street from us in a house behind a lot of trees, came up to the bus-stop and was startled when I said to her: 'I'm coming with you this morning, Mrs Fogg, my mother said I should.' And off we sailed in the bus towards yet another Pure Land with yet another arcane language to master. I was to live there, on and off, for several decades, and part of me still does. It's the most bracingly atheistic religion I've ever encountered, apart from Buddhism. It's not a matter of belief, it's a matter of being at home.

Indeed, it wasn't, I found, a religion that encouraged belief of any kind and I've mistrusted belief ever since. It encouraged understanding, but not in easy cosmic steps ('On Friday night in the Masonic Hall, Smith St, Mrs Jorgensen will explain the Third Circle of Seeing. Light refreshments will be served'—none of that). The approach was much more restrained and Buddhistic, reflecting through some convoluted genealogy Buddhism's profound critique of materialism—not that that is how it's generally perceived in the community at large. It didn't take me long to realise that almost everyone saw it as the religion of daffy aunts and Doris Day, the sort of nutters whose cats died because they wouldn't take them to the vet—and worse. One Sunday morning Tom was out the back cleaning shoes in the sun and talking to his sister Eva who was over from Adelaide. We were all a bit in awe of Eva because she'd had Money since her husband had died and she'd been to the Coronation on it. She used to show us albums of photographs of herself in front of Catholic churches in cities all over the world. There in the backyard Tom told Eva where I was off to that morning (Eva had been back from Mass for hours) and she was thunderstruck. 'He's not!' she said, staggered. 'Why do you let him?' And I sat on the back steps, shoeless, and listened to Eva, who was almost in tears, remonstrating with her brother and to Tom humming and the swish of the shoebrush until finally she said: 'Look, I'll pay to send him to St Ignatius. I'd be happy to.'

Well, this was more interesting. I knew nothing about class, but I knew a toffy school when I saw one. And I'd seen St Ignatius above the bay on the Lane Cove River many times on my late-afternoon walks with the dog (thinking very hard, at that time, about the ultimate unreality of anything that was not God). It would be a definite step up. But when Jean caught whiff of it, she became quite white-faced. On no account would her son go to a Catholic college. Secretly, apart from the betrayal of the clan, she must have had in mind her golden rule that one should know one's station. You'd only be humiliated if you forgot yourself. She'd seen ample proof of that. Like the time she'd invited all the neighbours to a New Year's Eve party and made cakes and put the china out—I'd cleaned the silver—and absolutely no one had come. She'd cried herself to sleep.

So that was the end of St Ignatius. I expect I just put on my clean shoes and went off to Sunday School to learn about God as Father-Mother, not just Father, what it could mean to say that 'man is made in the image and likeness of God', why matter as we think of it cannot coexist with God and all sorts of other exciting things no one ever talked about anywhere else. Except for Tom, on the back verandah or cutting back the lantana, but he used to get so waffly and theosophical—I wanted something more strenuous and disciplined.

This particular island of thought suited me well for many reasons. In the first place it was an overwhelmingly feminine world, discovered and charted by a woman who was extraordinary in anyone's terms, at its centre was a Mother Church and in its daily ministerings it spoke to me above all through women, from Sunday School teachers to the church leaders on the other side of the world. I felt unanxiously and securely mothered.

Not that Jean was an unloving mother—quite the contrary. But she loved me as a kind of exotic plant she'd promised faithfully to tend, one that showed early signs of getting out of hand. When I visited school friends, I used to sense that something about the way they were loved by their mothers was different. They seemed to be loved by their mothers more robustly, more moistly than I was, the bonding seemed to be more taken for granted, more elastic, allowing for explosions of anger, for jibes and displays of affection we'd have found embarrassing or even paralysing. Jean's loving was grateful and self-doubting. It was hedged about with a bewildered hurt at how arid life had become, how nothing seemed to take root, how everything she felt drawn to seemed to dry up and die. Even now, when I try to focus on Jean's failed life, I want to turn away and think about something else. She'd married Tom the sailor, dashing in a plumpish way in his white uniform, in Perth in 1927, when she was a 26-year-old nurse and his ship was in Western Australian waters for a time. Twenty years later there seemed to be affection—they were both good people—but not love between them. Jean read good books from the library, took me to the theatre to see plays and ballet from Over There—*The Caucasian Chalk Circle*, for example, Martha Graham and the Borovansky Ballet. She yearned for close friends and sometimes, I think, for passion. She wanted a companion who could talk about ideas and feelings, pined (I see it all quite clearly now) for beauty, in small things like tea-cups and bigger things, like what it all meant. Instead she lived with a fat man in baggy shorts who told funny stories, never read a book except for his dog-eared French textbook, thought *Gigi* and *South Pacific* at the local cinema on a Saturday night were 'culture' enough for any man, and lived life as it came. The house was poky and unfinished, no one much seemed to visit, except very occasionally for an old nursing friend or two of Jean's from the West. (Tom only had one friend, who lived in Melbourne.) The tea-cups came from jumble sales and we even had to take in a boarder for a while to make ends meet, Tom being just a clerk in a cables office. (I thought it the most exciting job in the world. Tom knew what time it was in Rio de Janeiro and Reykjavik, people came into his office and sent urgent messages to New York and Colombo. I used to boast about it at school until I learnt that a father who was a 65-year-old clerk at the end of his career was not something you drew attention to.) Jean did have one beautiful thing: a brilliantly coloured bowl by Clarice Cliff, perfectly round like a blue-and-pink che-quered ball. It goes everywhere with me.

Before I came to live with them, Jean had had a nervous breakdown. From what I could gather, a nervous breakdown was a shameful illness women were prey to and you spoke about it in hushed tones. It was a dark cloud that just sat on the horizon all through my childhood, until one day it blew over again and everything went dark for a long time. All I really knew about it was that for about two years Jean had not been able to leave the house and had washed her hands obsessively until they were red-raw. If I were not very good, it might happen again. All that yearning, all that high-mind-edness, all that banality and dead-end ordinariness—it was quite Chekhovian in its way, which is why I found Chekhov almost too painful to read at first and declared him 'boring'.

By way of contrast my new religious family gave signifi-cance to life's minutest detail—'the very hairs of your head are all numbered', not one sparrow falls 'without your Father'. It had an appealing order and serenity to it, independent of human personalities. There were no priests or popes or even boring parish worthies to foist their ratty views on you. There were just the Books. It was all so universal, too—in Delhi and Helsinki, in Warsaw and Nairobi, the vision and the words and the service and the Books were just the same. It was dependent on language, exegesis, interpretation, study and, most importantly for me, it was thoroughly Protestant (in an intriguingly Buddhist sort of way). It was perfect. It was very Pure.

Well-wishers, anxious about my spiritual welfare, slipped me pamphlets and booklets by learned antagonists such as the historian H.A.L. Fisher. Dr Leslie Weatherhead was another one, I remember, and a friend from school found a particularly vicious little tract for me by a Dr Rumble in a rack in St Mary's Cathedral. Their concern, naturally enough, was for the purity of their own orthodox brand of Christianity, concocted in the fourth century in Asia Minor to an imperial agenda, the source of immense power and wealth for millions of men over the intervening millenium and a half. They were also concerned to suggest that while a woman might properly be a saint, she had no business founding a church and running its affairs. She must have been either a charlatan or mad or possibly both. None of this was my concern at all, so I never found what they had to say (much of it seething with a strikingly unChristlike hatred) of much interest. All I wanted to know was: did it work? Eventually, when the evangelist Billy Graham came to Australia in 1959, my next-door neighbours gave me a copy of his *Peace with God.* I read it with great attention and it proved a turning-point for me. After reading *Peace with God* I turned my back on mainstream Christianity for good. As Turgenev has written, a religion that teaches that God sent himself in the form of his own son down to earth to offer his other sons salvation by sacrificing himself to himself—well, it's too silly, really, to spend time even completing the sentence. I had better things to do with my time.

❖ ❖ ❖

You're thinking, I'm sure, among even less charitable things, that I'd have done much better to be out on the street being homosocial, kicking footballs, fighting, teasing girls and so on, like normal little boys. Or if I *had* to sit about inside dreaming, I ought at least have read Biggles books or played with my Meccano set or something. Well, I was different. I just didn't feel the need. And it gets worse.

For some reason, when I was still quite small—perhaps ten

or eleven—I went into the local papershop and bought
myself a little Russian dictionary. Perhaps it was the script that
intrigued me, perhaps the wickedness, the illicitness of anything Russian. I knew about the Russians, you see, because
Tom had told me about them while shaving one morning in
our cramped bathroom. I'd asked him what Communism
was (because we were all obsessed with fighting it) and he'd
told me that in Communist countries everyone had to wear the
same shoes and clothes and do what the government told
them to do. This was easy to grasp and quite appealed, in a
way. It appealed to the neat-edged lawn/God as the ultimate Lawgiver side of my nature, the side which dreamt
sometimes of turning the wild gully at the back of the
house into a landscaped park and getting rid of the blue-
tongues in our lantana.

So I sat not on the back verandah, with the bush crowding
in, but at a bridge-table on the front verandah by the begonia-
boxes to study my *Collins English-Russian Russian-English
Dictionary*, with its fake morocco binding and sensuous
Bible paper covered in illicit script. You can't learn much from
a dictionary, of course, but at least the little square script
grew familiar, and after a while I wanted to build something with the words. So, at seven o'clock one Tuesday
evening at the WEA in Phillip Street, I set my sights on a
third Pure Land, the most chimeric of all: Russia, Mother
Russia, with her own intoxicating language. Each of the
three began to colour the other two (my private language
became peppered with Slavic roots, for example, and I

pored over Russian translations of my religious texts) but this third Pure Land went on to dominate my life long after I'd stopped believing in it.

Mrs Z, my teacher, was unlike any woman I'd ever met. Aunty Eva and her Coronation, artistic Aunty Moat, my fading, anxiety-ridden mother Jean—they all paled into insignificance beside her. To me, at the beginning, she was a kind of princess. She was mysteriously exotic, coming as she did from Manchuria with stories of gay picnics in the gardens of the summer palaces. She often dressed at home in what I thought of as silks and brocades from the East, right down to the floor, and she would come hurrying upstairs after our lesson with dishes I'd never set eyes on: strange sharp-tasting fish, fat pancakes spread with caviar, gigantic tortes covered in cream and strawberries, and tea, of course, endless cups of stewed black tea from a real samovar. There was a pleasing autocratic streak in Mrs Z as well, the sense she gave that this was how things were done, that nothing else would do and that the natives would simply have to be badgered and cajoled into doing things her way. And down in the basement, hidden away and never mentioned, like some scruffy house-spirit, lived a shabby, shambling man. I never found out exactly who this creature was. Perhaps a husband.

Like exiled aristocrats in reduced circumstances ever-where in the world Mrs Z was privately scathing about the country that had taken her in. Culture, poetry, literature, music, fine cuisine, sophisticated conversation—it all resided over there somewhere, not precisely in Manchuria, of course, which for some obscure reason she'd chosen to leave, and not precisely in Moscow, where she'd never been, but certainly not here. I could only take her word for it.

I learnt very fast. You do at that age. Not only were there the evening classes at the WEA, but also weekly lessons on the closed-in verandah of her house in North Sydney with its spectacular view over roofs and backyards to the bridge and the harbour. I learnt not only to recite Lermontov's romantic verse by heart and to read short stories by Tolstoy and Chekhov, but also about justice and freedom and equality in a land where some entity called 'the people' owned everything, no one was rich or poor, everyone from bus-drivers to atomic scientists laboured for the common good, nature was the happy servant of Man, various ethnic minorities engaged in fruitful exchanges with other ethnic minorities, forming colourful, noisy dance troupes, and, most importantly, no one wanted war. The disappointingly smudgy pictures in the books and magazines we read seemed to bear out what Mrs Z told me of her distant realm. The neat sketches in our textbooks, too, showed peaceful, happy families in spacious, square apartments, clean-cut tractor-drivers ploughing black fields and manly engineers damming rivers and building skyscrapers. Quite a few of the other students at the WEA seemed to think it made a lot of sense, too—writers, journalists, teachers, dancers with their hearts set on the Bolshoi, they all seemed to believe this was where the future lay. They certainly understood a lot more about the rottenness of the Australian political and economic system than I did.

The night we all rushed out into the street to gaze up at the first sputnik seemed to confirm the tales my princess had been telling me. Science was conquering not just the Earth, but the cosmos as well and Science spoke Russian. True, it was Godless Science, but God had promised man dominion over the fish of the sea, and over the fowl of the air, and over the cattle, and over all the earth, had He not, and perhaps, in the fullness of time, and after many overturnings, my two Pure Lands might find they were one.

I must say I had my doubts about the literal truth of Mrs Z's message right from the start, not, of course, that I expected princesses to concern themselves overmuch with mere literal truths. Mrs Z would marshal me occasionally into mixing with Australian believers in her everlasting kingdom—if you've ever belonged to a fringe grouping of some kind, you'll immediately know the kind of thing I mean: we might spend the day picnicking with sailors from a Russian ship, for example, or watch a film about partisans in a forest in a hall with uncomfortable chairs—and I couldn't help noticing even then that there was something not quite right about them, something that made me feel ill at ease, the sort of feeling you can get when Jehovah's Witnesses ring on the doorbell and ask you if you're concerned about Armageddon. It wasn't just that there was a sprinkling of physical deformities—wall-eyes, withered hands, overwhelming body odour and so on, although this put you on your guard—it was more the sense that for these people nothing just *was*, everything had to be reinterpreted and reclassified, every story had to be retold with a different ending. We'd be driving our sailors through Turramurra on our way to the picnic grounds by the water at Bobbin Head, for example, enjoying the gardens, the lushness, the peace, the colours, the bush, and all of a sudden I'd be asked to explain to the sailors in Russian that this was where the exploiting class lived, these houses and gardens were built on the blood and sweat of the workers, and this church (however charming it may look to their innocent eyes with its un-Russian steeple and frangipani blossoms dripping over the fence) was just an arm of an international conspiracy to lull the workers into ... The sailors never said a word, I noticed, not a syllable, and seemed faintly bored, I thought, at Bobbin Head. It was a huge relief in Russia years later to find that no one I met really believed these retold stories, any more than children really believe the Creeds. They may have repeated them, they may have said 'yes' to the question 'do you believe them?' but, except in adolescence, these stories never related to the real world. But in this absurd world of make-believe I was hovering on the fringes of, as in any dogmatic belief system, it was thought that if you said the sky was green often enough and with enough conviction, everyone would agree it was green and so, finally, to all intents and purposes, it would be. And if a few million human beings had to die in the process, well, as Mrs Z used to say, looking out on the world from her tower in North Sydney, when you chop wood, chips fly. Wherever adolescence is arrested (in churches, tertiary institutions, men's clubs, political parties) it remains a popular view. Whether it's called lefitst or rightist depends, naturally enough, on which way you're facing.

It's hard to find the right word to describe our relationship, Mrs Z's and mine. In middle-class Australian society there's a limit to the number of rôles a middle-aged woman with few ties can have to an unrelated adolescent boy. She can be a teacher (as Mrs Z partly was) or a friend of the family, an 'auntie' (which she never quite became—Jean and Tom found her too outlandish and she found they smacked too much of the common herd) or a neighbour, but not much else. Mrs Z, in a society which had no place for such an office, saw herself, I think, as a kind of duenna, chaperoning me as I stepped out into the world, guiding me with a knowing hand away from misalliances into circles she approved of.

Our first real rift occurred over the Berlin Wall years later, in 1965. When it first went up in 1961 I remember clearly one of Mrs Z's friends explaining to me with what I can only call a sort of strident patience that it was we in the capitalist West who were behind the barbed wire and those in the East who were free and outside it. The Wall, it turned out, had been built to keep the fascist warmongers in the West out, while the good folk in the East went about their peace-loving, non-exploitative business. If I didn't like being locked in behind walls, barbed wire and machine-gun turrets, then I should head East just as soon as I could—there were ways. Indeed there were—travel agencies in Pitt Street, for example—and I did, in 1965. I went to Berlin.

I flew in from Munich. Flying in in those days minimised

the impact. Years later Peter and I went from Munich to Berlin by train. Peter fell silent almost as soon as we crossed the border of the GDR at Hof and as we trundled north under a yellowish sky through the devastated landscape of the GDR, through those surreally silent, grimy towns straight out of Victorian England, Peter, a mild-mannered, politically undogmatic man, fell ill with tension and a kind of grief.

But on that autumnal afternoon in 1965 I approached the Wall with a certain amount of confidence. I'd just spent a few days in Beverly Hills in California, safe in a secluded mansion stuffed full of Meissen figurines while Watts went up in flames on the other side of Los Angeles, and also on Manhattan, squeezed in with student friends in a tiny apartment on West 56th Street. Los Angeles and New York seemed to confirm what I'd been suspecting: that the capitalist world was indeed divided into exploiters and the exploited and the result was rat-infested slums, violence and millions of mutilated lives. I had not been seduced by a stroll down Fifth Avenue.

I think it was near Potsdamer Platz that I first caught sight of the Wall. You had to walk up to it across scarred vacant land. I climbed up the wooden stairs to the landing and peered across at a watch-tower and some nondescript, brownish apartment blocks on a street just a few yards away. Just out of sight behind those apartments a tram screeched as it turned a corner. Otherwise it was all as lifeless as a stage-set. I've never forgotten the screeching tram, lost somewhere in the October fog a street or two away, because as it screeched, precisely at the moment it clanked and screeched, I had another of my luminous moments. It was as plain as the nose on your face that *I* was not behind the Wall, *they* were. The prison was over there, after all. That was nearly thirty years ago now, yet to this day every tram that screeches as it turns a corner, even the East Brunswick turning into Bourke Street, Melbourne, seems to be warning me against belief and humbug.

I didn't cross the Wall until the next morning on the S-Bahn, curving across the sinister walled canal into Friedrichstrasse station's glassy hall. Up in the rafters were armed guards and hidden down below at street level manning the checkpoint was a squad of Hollywood Nazis called the Grenzsoldaten. As you stepped from the train in those days onto the platform where Westerners could change trains and head back to the West on another line or take the stairs down to street-level to enter East Berlin, you saw the platform divided lengthwise down the middle by an opaque glass wall. On the other side, not a metre away, you could make out the silhouettes of people living in another world, forbidden to enter yours. It was almost unbearably, ecstatically exciting. For me it was like stepping outside myself into a simulacrum of my own brain, if I can put it that way. My inner world had in a flash become the outer because there in front of me—I could touch it—just a centimetre thick was the division between ordered paradise and the jungle, between system and chaos, between heaven coming to pass and real life. Or so we were told. The ultimate icon. I hurried downstairs, paid my ten Deutschmarks, pushed open a swing door and found myself in a real Pure Land.

It was, as you'd expect, exactly like all the others I was to visit that October and in later years, in Czechoslovakia, Hungary, Poland, Romania, Bulgaria and, of course, Russia. They even smelt the same. They're well documented. You don't need me to tell you about them. They weren't pure. They had no hope of being pure. They were built for angels by people who didn't even believe in angels.

I'd smuggled in some journals and magazines that October morning past the chilling Nazi lookalikes about a different kind of paradise and caught a tram into the suburbs way out towards the north-east to pass them on to people whose address I'd been given. Hitler's laws about minority religions (sects, we like to call them in English, to establish our disdain for them) had been kept intact by the regime in the GDR and the least I could now do was to contravene them. I did this for years in all sorts of places—Russia, Lithuania, Hungary, Czechoslovakia—in fact, at one point I had quite a little network operating out of Moscow through Sergei Prokofiev's wife Lina Ivanovna. Smuggling for God brought me into contact with all sorts of eccentric, courageous, intelligent people with enormous strength of character, despised, of course, both there and here as daft if not stark raving mad, but just for the record I'd like to say that they struck me almost without exception, and still strike me, as amongst the most clear-sighted people I've ever had dealings with.

Mrs Z was furious when I got back to Sydney and told her what I thought of the Wall. She quivered with displeasure. It was our first serious disagreement and a harbinger of things to come. The Germans, she told me, richly deserved any minor inconvenience such as a wall that might come their way. In fact, what they deserved was suffering on a much grander scale altogether. And if life in the Soviet sector was a little greyer than life in the American sector, that was historically understandable and in the fullness of time would change. America, as always, was obscurely to blame for the Wall, for the difference in living standards and for the temporary limitations on individual freedom in the GDR. I could follow her argument, but I caught the whiff of bad faith and it never quite left my nostrils.

Not long ago, in another foggy October, I caught a bright yellow double-decker bus (No. 100) from Berlin Zoo just off the Kurfürstendamm straight past the Reichstag, through the middle of the Brandenburg Gate to the corner of Unter den Linden. I could hardly believe what I was seeing through the front window of the bus—we simply swung right at the Reichstag into Ebertstrasse (once cut off from the West by the Wall) and then veered left straight through the middle of the Brandenburg Gate. This wasn't me, this wasn't the twentieth century. I jumped out into it. There on the pavement on Pariser Platz in the chilly sunshine is a bazaar. Once you'd have been shot for standing there. Now Russians and Tamils and Rumanians are huddled there selling Soviet sailors' caps, matryoshka dolls, red and gold Lenin badges and little banners which read: 'We shall arrive at the victory of Communist labour!' Just Soviet bric-à-brac now, thrown in with the chocolate bars and belts and scarves and maps of Berlin. It should be exhilarating, but it's unbearably banal. I can't look at it for long. I walk off eastwards up Unter den Linden past the Yamaha showrooms.

In the mid-sixties it was unimaginable that I could live to see this. A divided Europe seemed a natural dialectical arrangement, a legitimate stage in the march of History. All the same, by 1965 I was to an extent my own man (or so I thought). I now had a degree in Russian and French from the ANU in Canberra and a Master's thesis in Soviet literature underway in the same department. I'd flown alone right around the world, visited a dozen countries, and not just France and Germany: I'd made my way across Czechoslovakia and Hungary, wandered about the streets of Calcutta, and gone cycling around the Kathmandu valley when there were few Europeans to be seen in Nepal. Guilt about leaving Jean and Tom to live their comfortless lives without me did nag at me, did distress me—I hadn't, after all, lived at home since moving to Canberra in 1962—but I assuaged the guilt by writing them long letters, full of intimate detail and assurances of my love. There was no reproach in their letters to me—there was no pleasure to compare with finding one of Tom's fat, loving letters waiting for me somewhere—but deep down I always had to do battle with the fear I'd abandoned them for selfish reasons, a cardinal sin in my book.

Mrs Z's watchful, mothering eye still followed me about in those years. It was becoming an irritation. My childhood princess was looking more and more like an ageing xenophobe in a cheong sam with Manchurian ideas about what had been going on in the world for the past fifty years and a disturbing tendency to shout 'Off with his head' when crossed. *'Rasstrelyat' nado!* ' ('They should be shot!') was an all too common reaction to any mention of people with dissident views, Pasternak was a talentless nincompoop, Solzhenitsyn a traitor, Akhmatova, Tsvetayeva and Gumilev beneath mentioning. It was time I went to Russia and confronted the reality.

As you can see, the self I packed off to Russia to confront the reality (the only one of my three Pure Lands to have a reality to confront) was not an archetypally Australian male self, if there is such a thing. It knew nothing about any kind of sport (I was forced to play football at school, but never learnt the rules and still don't know what sort of football it was), had never held a cricket bat in its hand or seen a horse-race, it had never gambled, not even ever bought a lottery ticket, it had never drunk alcohol (in fact, my experience of alcohol is still limited to one glass of Veuve Clicquot, which, if you're interested, tastes to a virginal palate like a very indifferent apple juice), it had never been in a pub, didn't know a Holden from a Rover and couldn't drive. It wasn't even an Australian intellectual in any real sense: it knew nothing to speak of about Australian politics or history—Archbishop Mannix, say, or Ben Chifley or the Eureka Stockade, these names evoked virtually nothing—and even less about Australian literature or painting (Nolan, Boyd, Williams, Tucker) which it had barely heard mentioned. It didn't even know it was living in the 'sixties. It's astonishing that I could have missed the 'sixties so completely, living in a university college, but I contrived to. Smoking dope, dropping acid, rock music festivals, *Rolling Stone*, Bob Dylan, Vietnam marches, Che Guevara posters—none of it meant anything to me at all. In Moscow a student I was friendly with asked me to translate some Dylan into Russian, but I couldn't because I didn't understand the English. No, I had no sense of any revolution sweeping over the world. Marijuana, Fidel Castro, Ho Chi Minh, the Rolling Stones—to me they were all just different faces of materialism on the march, different forms of the same old authoritarian message: don't try to think, you are just a biochemical reaction in *our* laboratory. So, you see, if anything, this prim little self, almost disconnected from any kind of social reality, with its head in Boston, St Petersburg, Paris, London, anywhere but here, thought *it* was the rebel, not Dylan or Che Guevara. And Moscow did not disillusion it.

CHAPTER THREE

Mother Russia

Mrs Z was nervously excited when I set off for Moscow for the first time in 1966 as an exchange student. On the one hand I was going to live in the Promised Land she'd never seen, but on the other hand I'd be unchaperoned and might misinterpret what I saw. Which from her point of view I did. Once I got there, it appeared to me that the capitalist press and its running dogs had actually got it all pretty right. Not quite right, perhaps—the reality was more Byzantine, more richly textured and more contradictory than *The Sydney Morning Herald* could be bothered with—but by and large Western right-wing propaganda seemed to have hit the nail on the head. And so had Tom, in a crude sort of way, shaving in the bathroom.

Mrs Z was not as naïve in her hopes, however, as a fellow student of mine in Moscow, an undergraduate from provincial Tula (Tolstoy country). He'd been told to attach himself to me for the usual reasons and, casting about for a pretext, he seized upon my ten-volume set of Dostoevsky. Every week for ten weeks he'd come to my room to borrow another volume and have a little chat, touching only very cursorily on Dostoevsky. He was dazzled by Moscow's monumental grandeur, the boulevards, the symmetrical vistas, the wedding-cake sky-scrapers (we lived in one on the Lenin Hills) and he used to ask me, with a touching, almost childlike awe in his voice, how I could live here, at the centre of world Communism, in this palace of learning set amidst parks on the hills above the river, not half an hour from Red Square on the futuristic underground, and still not believe. Surely this was the Third Rome. I didn't quite know what to say to that, and after he'd returned the tenth volume of Dostoevsky the University's Foreign Department started sending someone else. I had the same trouble in Lourdes once when my companion on a bus tour, an Irishwoman from Galway, was similarly hurt and amazed that I could be there, in Lourdes, at the grotto and in the church, and still not believe. I'd wanted to say to her, and wanted to say to my friend from Tula, that it was precisely *because* I was there at the shrine that belief was impossible—and understanding became imperative.

Things got off to a bad start in Moscow. I arrived there in summer clothes almost straight from Marrakech expecting to find a suitcase of warmer clothes I'd sent ahead waiting for me at the Embassy. To my astonishment the case had been stolen from the First Secretary's office. The two Moscow policemen put onto the job insisted someone at the Embassy had stolen it. The idea was so ludicrous I couldn't understand how they could keep a straight face. But then, of course, they weren't policemen, they didn't believe the story, either, and would have had contempt for me if they'd thought I believed it. In some sort of sense they'd stolen it themselves, probably, or had been told who had. The important thing was to fill out the forms, mouth the right regrets and hopes, shake hands and go about our business. If we all agree the sky is green, then it must be.

I never saw the case again, and the first month was a bit of a strain—the weather turned raw early, people were officious and rude, and in the student cafeteria the food was for the most part abominable and all the knives had been stolen. My main memory of mealtimes is of sitting in a cavernous dining hall shovelling mashed potato and gravy into my mouth with a bent fork. Everything seemed to turn into a saga, from registering at the library to having a friend come to my room on a simple visit. But at the end of the month, in early October, I had a watershed experience and felt a lot more relaxed. I'd gone up to the Foreign Department to talk about the course I was taking and to get permission for a friend to visit me in my room in the hostel. (For this you needed to make application in writing well in advance and the friend, in order to get through the two checkpoints, one at the gate and one inside the building, had to be armed with identification and a signed pass.) Things were going badly. I was looked after, if that's the right term, by Lilia Pavlovna, a completely charmless woman with badly dyed hair who was in charge of what they called the *krupnye kapitalisty*, an odd expression which means 'major capitalists' with overtones of grossness. It was flattering but not reassuring.

Lilia Pavlovna, adjusting from time to time both her teeth and her spectacles, was trying to convince me that it was in my best interests to study not Soviet literature, the area I was writing my Master's thesis in and had come to the Soviet Union specifically to work on, but Dostoevsky. I tried to reason with her. She had what Russian friends of mine called 'Soviet eyes', not just glassy but *osteklenevshie glaza*, 'eyes that have turned to glass'. There was no glimmer of human feeling or warmth in them at all. And the invitation to my room was a problem as well. Why was I inviting an American newspaper correspondent to my room? How did I know her? Where had we met? Then all of sudden I started to cry. I cried softly at first, a few tears trickling down my cheeks, and then I began to cry quite loudly and to shudder and heave and rock on my chair. I cried noisily and steadily for quite a few minutes. Lilia Pavlovna went rigid with shock. 'Take yourself in hand!' she said eventually through her ill-fitting teeth. 'Why are you crying? Calm yourself!' I didn't calm myself at all, but cried on and on in an ecstasy of release. Then I went downstairs to my room and cried on for about three hours. It may not have been the manly thing to do, but it was deeply cathartic. After that I felt ready to live in Moscow.

Lilia Pavlovna won, of course, but by then I didn't mind. One day the cloakroom attendant at the university library said: 'They've written something about you in the paper.' And indeed 'they' had. A small article had appeared in the weekly news magazine *Nedelya* explaining to its readers that the Australian authorities had sent to Moscow an exchange student with anti-Soviet ideas about Soviet literature and that this could not be tolerated. There was a quote from a Soviet professor who'd met me at the ANU in Canberra and found my views totally outlandish. (No such conversation had ever taken place.) The same week this article appeared, the good professor and I met on a marble staircase in the old university building in the centre of the city. He was sweeping down and I was in the milling crowd at the bottom in the damp. (Russian vestibules are always damp. There's always a sort of foul steam in the air.) He hailed me from several steps above. 'The Australian!' He was jovial today and looking very *soigné* as usual. Like apparatchiks everywhere, he was basically a large zero, a blank space, and, like Chichikov in *Dead Souls*, he could fill the space with whatever cardboard cutout of a man circumstances required—the grandfather, the thug, the roué, the romantic—it didn't matter.

'Well, we've talked about your case,' he said, swivelling in his fine silk suit to nod at this one and that, 'and decided you'll study Dostoevsky while you're here. With your attitudes to Soviet literature it's inappropriate for you to work here in that field. Dostoevsky.' He beamed. 'Agreed?'

It wasn't a question. In the event, I was grateful to Professor Kuleshov for plunging me into Dostoevsky for a whole year. In 1966 Dostoevsky had only just been rehabilitated and for the first time since the early years of the Revolution it was possible to discuss Dostoevsky's Christianity and novels like *The Devils* freely. I say 'freely', but I don't mean by this that all was permitted. In our weekly tutorials with Mr Tiunkin, a frightened rabbit of a man, terrified the Canadian or Australian in his class might suddenly come out with a heresy he'd then have to deal with, we'd begin with a short lecture on one of Dostoyevsky's novels or short stories, or perhaps on a chapter in Bakhtin's analysis of Dostoyevsky. (Bakhtin had also only just been rehabilitated and his, to us then, revolutionary book *Dostoyevsky's Poetics*, first published in 1929, had only just been republished in a miniscule print-run.) Then the class would have what was called a debate. Tiunkin would announce a proposition (for example, 'The figure of Raskolnikov is anti-revolutionary'), appoint one student to defend it and one to oppose it, and then at the end of the tutorial he, Tiunkin, would tell us who was right and who was wrong and why. It was freedom of sorts. The class paper we had to write on Dostoevsky was less 'free': it had to be couched in strictly Marxist literary terms and the bibliography had to begin with the letter L for Lenin, then go on to M for Marx, E for Engels and only then to A, B etc. No one minded or thought it odd. We were just giving unto Caesar. Much the same thing happens today in Australian tertiary institutions, after all, where, if not in the bibliography, at least in the text, we find the obligatory mention of Kristeva, Said, Foucault, Lacan, Irigaray ... We just have a wider range of orthodoxies struggling for dominance here—and the public's indifference to all of them is not concealed, just ignored.

Dostoevsky had a profound effect on my thinking—especially *Notes from Underground* and *Crime and Punishment*—despite the fact that if we'd ever met we would no doubt have disagreed about virtually everything. He posed all the modern questions in such a way that they came and savaged you in the night, he tortured you until your rationality crumbled and you were willing to give play to your own dualities. Polyphonic, he forced you to listen to your own polyphonies. I would find my various little catholicisms cowering in the corner. At least for a time. When you read, say, 'The Legend of the Grand Inquisitor' in *The Brothers Karamazov* , it's astonishing how true both voices ring, both Christ's and the Inquisitor's, how seductive they both are, how you yearn for both to be right: Christ, who loves humanity and for whom goodness must be freely chosen, even if this means some will chose evil, and the Inquisitor, who distrusts and despises humanity and for whom goodness must be imposed by force, by 'the sword of Caesar', through miracle, mystery and authority. Unfortunately, Dostoevsky is a poor prism for political and ethical ideas nowadays. In my final years of teaching Russian literature I found many students barely knew who Jesus Christ was, let alone what the Grand Inquisitor might represent. A few didn't know the difference between Christmas and Easter.

Every Wednesday I'd send off a letter to Jean and Tom, telling them everything—who I'd met, what I'd eaten, what plays or concerts I'd been to, what excursions were planned—long, overly bright letters, letters which said: 'Your son is investing his talents wisely, your sacrifice is worthwhile.' Once or twice a letter went astray. One day when I went to the University post office to collect my mail, one of the clerks handed me back a letter I'd posted the day before to Jean and Tom, still in its envelope but with the stamps missing. 'I'm sorry, but the postmaster sometimes steals the stamps,' the clerk said to me in a matter-of-fact sort of way. 'You'll have to buy some more and send it again.' So I did. Usually the mail got through, despite the postmaster's eccentricities, and Tom saved every letter and postcard, carefully numbered and dated, and replied every week in his squarish hand in long, rambling letters of his own. *Dear Robert, Pleased to have your letter of 20th November describing the parade you attended. It sounds most impressive. I'm glad you were well rugged up. It's getting quite warm here, the kikuyu is going mad, will have to get the Victa onto it again this weekend. Clarrie Harrison's leg is playing up on him again, he says it's the heat ...* Never the slightest hint of anxiety, never the faintest note of embarrass-ment that a son of his should be studying in Russia. Young men went away adventuring—that's what they did. He'd been in Vladivostok himself before the Revolution. Jean rarely wrote. She wept a lot, I gather, because her life was put-tering out incomprehensibly. She was completely uncom-panioned. Occasionally she'd add a jagged line or two or send a page in different inks, commenting on my letters in a fragmented sort of way. She was teetering now on the edge of her long slide into madness. When Tom finished building his cottage on the hill by the sea at Gerringong—beach, headlands and ocean on one side, deep misty-green valleys and mountains on the other—and they moved there from Sydney, she toppled right over the edge.

Often apologetically, people still ask me, decades later, what it was *like* living in Russia in the late 'sixties. In a word, it felt like entropy in action, if that's not an oxymoron. Organisation becoming disorganisation in front of your very eyes. It often felt as if you'd been caught up in the machinations of some provincial amateur dramatics society, where all the energy goes into arguing about who's a member and who isn't, what colour to paint the hall, who will design the programs and who has a right to the society's car—but no plays are ever put on, or only if the president writes them. It felt like Chekhov.

It also felt as if there was a war going on, which in a way there was, so it was depressing and dangerous and exciting all at the same time. As in any society at war, the State was glorified, nationalism was rampant, the culture was xenophobic (while posing as internationalist) and the press seethed with hatred of the enemy (Great Britain, the USA, West Germany, China), exaggerating reports of his imminent defeat. All dealings with the outside world—trips, telephone calls, reading the foreign press—were restricted and regarded with suspicion, everything down to the last bus-ticket and theatre program was censored, the architecture was overwhelmingly symmetrical, monumental and intimidating, the people spoke with one voice, individuals were mistrusted, the whole world with the exception of a few right-wing ruling cliques was on our side, the leader was compassionate, wise, ruthless, righteous, omnipotent, invincible, invisible ... It could've been any country at war.

A Mother's Disgrace

That's what it was *like*. It was my first conscious experience of the power that grows out of binary constructions of the world (in this case capitalist/socialist, exploiting/non-exploiting, truth/lies, enemy/friend—those were the main ones). It made me aware of the way binary constructions raise the stakes in any power game and make the thinking on both sides of the divide (the source of all power) more and more totalitarian.

It seemed natural, in this state of war, that food supplies should be erratic, that greens should disappear in winter, that cafés should run out of coffee and bakeries of bread. Given the times, new buildings were naturally gerry-built just as old buildings were shabby and overcrowded. Even at the university people worked in corridors, behind partitions or twenty to a room with classes for a dozen students held in oddly shaped cubicles the size of a suburban bathroom. Some of my friends lived in mysterious communal flats, with an assortment of other citizens crammed into the maze of rooms around them, their belongings spilling out into the dark passageway, the toilet, the bathroom, even the kitchen, an air of hostility and mistrust seeping into every corner of the flat. Not all my friends lived like that, of course. As in any war, hierarchies were crucially important. There were chains of command, as there had to be, and those issuing commands at the top needed a better view than those carrying them out at the bottom. And they got it: better housing, food, hospitals, medical services, shops, transport and schools. Soviet society seemed to me more rigidly layered than Ancient Egypt.

The layering was brought home to us very sharply as soon as we registered at the Lenin Library, which is where most of the foreign humanities students were to spend most of their days. As capitalist foreigners we were given passes to Room One, comfortably appointed with private desks and reading lamps and, most importantly, a special catalogue with references to holdings other catalogues in the library did not acknowledge existed. Along with our fellow readers in Room One from the Soviet academic élite, we did not line up in the morning for up to an hour to hand in our coats and scarves in the cloakroom, nor did we jostle for positions at overcrowded tables or wait hours for books to be delivered. It was some weeks before I discovered there was also a Room Two for the slightly less highly placed and politically reliable, a Room Three and even a Room Four for comrades with no status at all and a catalogue to cater to their limited needs. It was the denizens of these halls I strode past in the morning to hand in my coat and scarf at the head of the queue. No one seemed to think it was a peculiar arrangement.

The main difference from our kind of pyramidal structure was that in Russia the one mafia ran everything. There in some real sense a single mafia sat in parliament, designed the dust-jackets, ran the television stations, issued exit visas, owned all the businesses, published the newspapers, decided on the menu in the restaurants, provided the courts with judges, devised courses in French literature, censored the movies, planned new towns, dammed the rivers and ran the church. Here these functions are spread more entertainingly amongst a whole plethora of mafias—unions, political parties, criminal gangs, committees, cabals of the wealthy, networks of so-called public servants, local councils and so on. Each system has its advantages and disadvantages. The thuggish thrive in both.

Under our system, it must be said, one mafia can call another mafia to account. Under the Soviet system in my day the mafia that ran everything could not be called to account. To a Westerner this could be terrifying. On several occasions, during encounters with the KGB, the mafia's hit-squad and intelligence service, this arbitrary, limitless power chilled me to the core.

On the train at the Finnish border, for instance, everything seemed calculated to terrify. As you approached the border through birch forests, nothing stirred. No foresters, wood-cutters or road maintenance crews, no hikers or strollers, no families out for the day for a spot of fishing or even farmers farming. The carriage was sealed and then, as you rumbled through this unpeopled landscape, each individual compartment was locked. Eventually the train ground to a halt in what seemed to be the middle of nowhere—a few huts, a watch-tower, no platform—and huge mirrors were rolled up and down alongside the train, searching, I suppose, for anyone concealed underneath. Dogs were patrolled up and down the line. Inside the carriage: dead silence. Then methodically, unhurriedly, two KGB border guards unlocked each compartment, entered, relocked it and began to interrogate the passengers and search their luggage. I did this trip several times in both directions in the 'seventies and the pattern never varied. At night it was even more terrifying, with blinding searchlights hanging in the blackness and no sound except for dogs barking.

It wasn't the interrogation itself that intimidated me or the way they would spend what seemed like hours reading the labels on records, perusing magazines, unrolling your underwear or taking your electric razor to pieces, muttering disconnected questions all the while about who, where, why, what—why do you come here so often? what is this made of? why are you going to Finland? ... No, what brought you out in a cold sweat was the certain sense that these mafiosi could take you outside and beat you up, charge you with drug-trafficking, throw you in jail, even shoot you up against the barbed wire, or, if they felt like it, send you back to Leningrad—they could do anything at all with absolute impunity. They could not be held to account. You were worth precisely nothing, zero. (The answer to the question 'Why do you come here so often?', by the way, was 'Because I like it here so much.' That seemed to stump them. It was obviously a lie in some basic sense, but it conformed at the same time to an official truth. *Ponyatno* ('I see') was the only reply I ever got to that one.)

Eventually, of course, you'd lurch into no man's land, stop for what seemed like hours again (had a command gone out to haul you all back and arrest the lot of you?) and then set off again for the station at Vainikkala on the Finnish side of the border. It was always bathed in light, with people walking up and down the platform, talking, smiling, even laughing. The buffet would be open selling yoghurt, cakes, apples, bananas, ham sandwiches, orange juice, chocolate milk ... Everyone would crowd in smiling and talking loudly, the assistant would say 'Can I help you?' and 'Thank you' and you felt, perhaps simplistically, but you did, that this is how life should be in a civilised country. Go two hundred metres and the war is over.

Oddly enough, twenty years later, when my closest Russian friend came to visit me in Sydney for the first time, after applying intermittently for about ten years for an exit visa, she said much the same thing. 'It's so *normal* here,' she said. 'This is how people should live.' Zealot friends of Mrs Z's took her on a tour of Redfern and a psychiatric hospital at Rozelle and tried to explain to her about late capitalism. 'No, no, you don't understand—this is all *normal*,' she kept saying, 'this is how human beings should live.' It isn't, of course, and any cultural materialist worth his salt should have been able to make it clear to her that 'normal' has no universal meaning, but I knew exactly what she meant after those border crossings into Finland.

The most sinister border crossing I ever made was in the other direction. We were rattling along in the train between the border and the first city on the Soviet side, Vyborg, once a Finnish city called Viipuri. This is where the border guards left the train in those days and I suppose took the bus home to be exemplary fathers and sons and husbands. I was sharing a compartment with a Belgian businessman who had made no secret of his Soviet sympathies. He was the son of Russian émigrés in Brussels, sleekly suited, suave in a Gallic sort of way. We pulled into the platform at Vyborg, empty except for men in uniform. We both stared out the window at the magnificent ornate woodwork on the doors opposite. Suddenly two KGB guards dragged a screaming woman off the train, across the deserted platform past our window and through the massive oak doors we were staring at. 'No, no, no!' she was screaming—what else was there to scream? 'Let me go! Let me go!' There was silence for a moment in our cosy compartment. Then, still gazing steadily out the window at the station, my companion said placidly: 'What beautiful doors!'

That remark was echoed a thousand times during my years in Russia. What a beautiful park! What a beautiful church! What a beautiful view! What a beautiful city! What delicious ice-cream! What a wonderful concert! All true. Yet, as with the doors at Vyborg, there was something vaguely obscene about saying so without mentioning the screaming woman. Not that you could, really, even with friends, any more than visiting Russians can decently bring up Aborigines dying blind and diseased at forty-five in humpies and shacks all over the country while they're on a shopping spree in David Jones. In normal intercourse the two realities must be allowed to coexist. Some Russian friends didn't want to talk about anything else except the screaming woman—about censorship, corruption, labour camps, geno-cide—and, although it sounds shameful to say so (because all

those things were going on) that became tedious, too.
Again, it was like the war—you couldn't think and talk
about suffering all the time.

You must remember that we foreigners lived like princes. It's
a wicked and wonderful feeling. Nowadays, I expect, you can
only really get that feeling by going to an underdeveloped
country in Africa or Asia and staying at the Hilton for a week or
two, venturing out into the teeming, smelly streets occasionally
in clean, ironed clothes to pick through souvenirs. Mrs Z was
certainly the princess when she first went to the Soviet
Union, long after I'd returned. Attired in fashionable silks
and wools and furs, she flew in with her matching bags
crammed full of expensive presents for her family and dis-
pensed largesse. A princess for three months. I think for Mrs Z
and other émigrés—even for me, if I'm honest— there's an element of regret in our joy that our Soviet friends can now
travel abroad and holiday in Heidelberg and buy Swatch
watches and videos ... and, well, live like princes and
princesses for a week or two as well. We've lost our cachet.

But in those days we were royalty. For a start, we had foreign passports so we could, if we felt like it, go to Paris for
Christmas or Helsinki for the weekend for some good food and
decadent living and bookshops you could browse in. And in
the end we'd fly off to our Shangri-las anyway, to countries
impossibly far away, forbidden, forever inaccessible, where
people lived unimaginably pleasurable lives. 'Abroad', 'over
there', *zagranitsa* ('across the border') was almost fetishised.
Bulgaria or the GDR might be technically over the border, but

they weren't *zagranitsa*. If you claimed to have been abroad and then revealed you'd only spent two weeks at some Rumanian seaside resort, you'd be showing yourself up for the hick you were. *Zagranitsa* meant the West.

People had funny ideas about what was 'over there', twenty-seven kingdoms away, as they say in Russian. Once, in a train to the east of Moscow, I found myself in a compartment with two young men going home from prison. They were handsome and brutal and ignorant. They were astonished to find themselves talking to someone from 'over there'. All I remember from our conversation was how outraged they were to learn that I didn't have a double-storeyed house or a car or a pool or take my vacations in Rio di Janeiro. They suspected I was a government stooge and the conversation turned quite nasty. On the other hand, an Estonian friend of mine, an academic who eventually made a visit to Denmark, was so overwhelmed by what he saw (a vision of Estonia as it might have been without Soviet occupation) that he had to go into therapy when he got back to Tallinn.

Apart from our passports, we had dollars. Dollars made all the difference. There were special shops in Moscow in those days that sold anything you might want from cameras to caviar, from cars to Akhmatova's poetry, for dollars. And just to add insult to injury, cheaply. So every week I'd go across town on the underground to the shop on Kutuzov Avenue and stock up on food that was unavailable elsewhere—apples and orange juice, veal cutlets, fine chocolate, jams and compotes, beans and cabbages—and then stagger off to Mrs

Prokofiev's flat upstairs in the same building to off-load some of it and talk about God (she always covered the telephone with a cushion just pro forma to foil the KGB) and then back to my room at the university on the Lenin Hills to cook up a decent meal. And dollars got us into the Bolshoi, dollars got us a table in a top-class restaurant, dollars got us out of almost any queue and straight in the door. Like princes.

Our attitude to Soviet legalities was princely as well. Since few of us regarded the regime in power as legitimate in any meaningful sense, few of us had much compunction about breaking Soviet law if we thought we could get away with it. There was a forty-kilometre limit on our movements, for example, unless we had a visa to pass beyond it, but most of us ignored the rules if they didn't suit us. I once took a bus to the Russian Orthodox monastery of Pechori over on the Estonian border, for instance, and clambered round the catacombs and talked with the priests, all without a visa, and in 1971 when I was in Moscow again with my wife, she went skiing with a friend in Armenia without a visa. Not that such expeditions were great threats to the Soviet State. A much more serious infringement of Soviet law was the smuggling of various kinds that most of us indulged in. I used to order all sorts of subversive books from Blackwells in Oxford and pick them up at the Australian Embassy on my weekly visits. Freud, Jung, Fromm, English and American fiction (it wouldn't have occurred to me to bring in Australian fiction), Bibles—and worse. I even managed to bring in Solzhenitsyn's *Cancer Ward* in a tiny Russian edition, printed specifically for smuggling, and all these books I gave to Russian friends who'd asked for them.

Along with the oranges and chocolates I used to take religious books and journals to Lina Ivanovna Prokofiev every week and she would arrange for them to be distributed to 'friends' in Leningrad, Vilnius and one or two other Russian cities. Lina Ivanovna was a rather crotchety, aristo-cratic, Latin personality (she was Spanish-born and eventual-ly became a Spanish citizen), obsessed with the question of which of the two Madame Prokofievs was the real Madame Prokofiev—she or the woman she referred to as Mendelson-Prokofieva. Prokofiev's wife, you see, received invitations to for-eign embassy receptions in Moscow, could prop up on the window-sill gold-embossed invitations to openings in London and Madrid, had entrée into certain privileged circles amongst Moscow's cultural élite—but which of the two women was she? Legally Lina Ivanovna was—Prokofiev never divorced her after taking up with Mira Mendelson-Prokofieva—but the Soviet government gave its preference to Mira, who had strong Party connections. I was disappointingly uninterested in the whole question, I think. It was too much like a Gogolian farce, and I much preferred to get on with our smuggling or to listen to her talk about her extra-ordinary life in Paris and America and about how, one after-noon on her way back from a Western embassy, she was arrested by the KGB and sent to a labour camp for eight years, about how her interrogators had taunted her, since she believed God was Spirit and was All, to turn herself into a bird and fly out the barred window, about how her children came home from school that afternoon to find the flat empty, the floor-boards ripped up, the wall-paper hanging in strips from the walls and their mother 'disappeared'.

One of the problems on the smuggling front was that none of our 'friends', especially in Leningrad or Vilnius, was quite in Lina Ivanovna's social class. She loved them in a touching sort of way because of the ideas they'd held onto in silence together through prison and concentration camp over decades, but they also irritated her with their ordinariness. They were nobodies, and in Russian culture this question of the nobody versus the somebody (of what makes an identity, what validates it) is one that's always been acutely felt. 'Who do you think you are?' the Madman's head of department asks in Gogol's *Diary of a Madman*. '*What* are you? Just nothing, an absolute *nobody*.' The Madman counters that the director is 'really a *cork*, not a director, and an ordinary cork at that—a common or garden cork, and nothing else ...' Without God, Gogol would have said, identity has no meaning. We're all just corks—or heads of departments or Kings of Spain, it makes no difference—without God. There's no up or down without an absolute indication of direction. I fear I may have said something similar to Lina Ivanovna about her own identity—I was not averse to bringing the conversation pompously back to basics. And although I'm sure she nodded in agreement and smiled and patted my hand, I don't imagine any metaphysical argument could have withstood the pressure of an invitation to the

United States Embassy, or her highly coloured sense of herself as Lina Llubera, Spanish concert singer, wife of Russia's most gifted composer.

You couldn't help loving our 'friends' in Leningrad. Sometimes one of them would come to Moscow to pick up the books and journals, sometimes I would go to them in Leningrad on some pretext. Any arrangement involved risky calls from public telephone booths to communal flats and, for Olga Aleksandrovna in particular, since she was blind, difficult journeys alone across town in buses and trams. We used to meet in Marya Timofeyevna's room in a flat on the top floor of an old palace right on the Neva, on the Kutuzov Embankment near Peter the Great's summer palace. We'd sit there, the three of us, looking out across the river to the Peter and Paul Fortress and the cruiser Aurora and warm each other with cups of tea and talk about people we knew and metaphysics.

Marya Timofeyevna was a large, wheezing, moon-faced woman, jolly, contented, badly dressed—the kind of Russian woman you can see on any bus or tram, clutching her bulky bags and pushing her way with loud determination towards the door. She wanted warmth and reassurance from our meetings, she wanted to hear the Books read again, in Russian, after all those years—nearly forty now since the authorities had rounded them all up, sent some off to prison and death and let some live on in silence. Olga Aleksandrovna was altogether different. A heavy woman, always in black, with her silver hair drawn back in a bun, Olga Aleksandrovna was one of those sent to a prison camp in Bashkiria in the Urals for belonging to an outlawed religious society. She stayed there, in prison and then in exile, for twenty-nine years, until the Khrushchev era of de-Stalinisation, and through malnutrition had lost her sight. She now lived in a communal flat in the suburbs of Leningrad, a pensioner, like her friend Marya Timofeyevna, without a single trace of bitterness or the slightest sense of loss or deprivation. It still astonishes me. She was the metaphysician of the two, drinking in our readings, debating their meaning with a Talmudic intensity, laughing with joy at each discovery of meaning, seeing in her blindness more than any of us.

It struck me then, during the late 'sixties and early 'seventies when I was moving back and forth between Moscow and Canberra, how little scope there is in polite company in Australia for talking without embarrassment about anything too metaphysical—fears and feelings and private philosophies. In Russia I used to feel, perhaps wrongly, that you could turn to the person next to you on a bus and say: 'What do you think about death, then?' and get into a very interesting discussion, probably with the whole bus. You couldn't do that in Australia. I rarely had conversations like that with my friends at home. I never seem to have them now. It's partly my fault—I get so impatient with whatever I think is humbug. In Russia impatience was a style, a way of confronting the world. There you could shout 'Drivel!' and 'Lies!' and no one sulked or broke off the discussion. I think my friends at home, and Jean and Tom, must have thought me awfully stiff-necked and self-righteous—and no doubt I was, but it was partly style.

Even today, sometimes—rarely, because the subject is nowadays in such poor taste—I hear the urbane and the knowing in our society, the high-school-debating-society rationalists of our popular culture, pour scorn on any philosophy that questions the absolute reality of matter. They're joined by physicists and chemists on a gleeful winning streak, suburban Anglicans, medical gurus—indeed, the entire chatting establishment. To them above all it's lunatic idealism, an offensive denial of the reality of human suffering, a middle-class refusal to confront the world's Auschwitzes, Biafras and Mogadishus, not to mention lesser evils—stomach cancer, cyclones, pig farms, acid rain or the truly disgusting life cycle of the mole-rat.

I know what they mean, I acknowledge that they've 'won' (they 'own the discourse') and that there's no answer to their objections that they would find remotely acceptable. But I do remember Olga Aleksandrovna. In practice, I must say, not knowing quite how to say it, it doesn't at all work out the way one might think. In practice, the educated Buddhist or Christian Scientist or Sufi mystic can be as involved in the world and the rational solving of its problems as a quantum physicist, for much the same reasons—and be enriched by the infinite view in both directions. Understanding Einstein or the uncertainty principle or experimenting with some unified theory of everything, whatever it's called, in one sense changes everything, but in another nothing at all. You can be obsessed by quarks and still love P. D. James, understand that time and space are aspects of the same thing and still worry about missing the train, understand God to be All and still join the Labor Party or work in a rape crisis centre. The cut-off point for involvement in the world changes from person to person. It's annoying that this should be so, but it is.

Quantum physicists have a cultural advantage, all the same, over out-and-out idealists, even if their critique of common-sense materialism is as disruptive and profound as any idealist's. They are *scientists*, thus safe from the attacks of rationalist societies who can get on with pouring scorn on spoon-benders, mind-readers and levitators, even if what they actually *say* is more confronting to common sense than the wildest idealism. In the late twentieth century respectable people ask questions of science, not spiritual philosophies; and philosophers, historians, linguists and even literary critics scamper to get inside the scientific fold. It's the only way to be taken seriously by people you take seriously. If you want to know what is true and what isn't, if you want to revolutionise your thinking about the universe, you read not Teilhard de Chardin or Paul Tillich (let alone, God help us, some New England nut-case like Mary Baker Eddy—I can almost hear you snorting), but Paul Davies, Stephen Hawking, Richard Dawkins or James Gleick. You might *just* get away with a spiritual nut-case if it's Third World or ancient enough—some Himalayan guru or St Teresa of Avila. The Orange People recruited some very unlikely inner-suburban graduates to their cause on this principle. But it's inconceivable to anyone with an education and a mortgage that materialism could be mistaken in its fundamentals, even if it shades acceptably into belief and speculation on its outer fringes, at the level of superstrings and parallel universes, for example. Western materialism is in its heyday. It's been my experience that fundamental doubts about the absolute reality of matter are best kept to yourself.

Late in the 'seventies I went looking for Olga Aleksandrovna again. The only way to trace someone in those days was by going to an Information kiosk on a street corner, poking your identity card through the window and then asking for the address or telephone number you needed. There were no (publicly available) telephone or street directories, and this way, of course, 'they' knew who was interested in whom. I startled the woman in a Moscow kiosk once by asking for the telephone number of the Peruvian Embassy, which was, of course, classified information. If you didn't know the number of the Peruvian Embassy you must *ipso facto* be the kind of person who had no right to know it, so what was I doing by asking? Was I a lunatic, a spy, an insolent prankster? Anyway, on this occasion, I hadn't seen Olga Aleksandrovna for several years, I was in Leningrad for just a day or two and very much wanted to see her again. I stood on the hard-packed snow peering up into the little window in the kiosk waiting for the address. 'That citizen is dead,' said the woman briskly. There was nothing to do but wander away and remember.

Another answer I remember giving about what it was *like* to live in the Soviet Union was that it made you cynical. I must have been asked in Russian because I remember saying just one word: *tsinizm* (cynicism). It's an unpleasant word, especially in Russian. It cancels out hope. It says, I don't believe your stories, I mistrust your motives, your truths are self-serving lies, good will not triumph, greed has already won. In Russia cynicism is lightened with humour, a delight in the paradoxical and in clownishly mocking hypocrisy and official pieties. It's leavened in Russia, too, with a rather sentimental belief in the grain of goodness to be found gleaming some-where in the filth, the image of Christ to be espied in the most piggish of countenances. The Russians also had the advantage Noam Chomsky has referred to of living inside a totalitarian society and therefore not needing political illusions. The regime simply *coerced* people into repeating its lies and pieties about peace and freedom and justice and all the other abstractions leftist and rightist ideologies smother us in. Belief was beside the point. In our sort of society, by way of contrast, in radical student clubs and the RSL, for instance, illusion is of the essence and its manufacture by those at the top who believe in nothing an important industry.

The sort of experience I had in Russia during the Brezhnev years colours your attitude towards Australian leftism. It sours you. It would be strange if it didn't. So, while I do understand the faith our leftist intelligentsia and working-class activists once put in the Soviet Union, particularly in the 1930s, and their eagerness to weigh in on the socialist side in what they saw as the battle between 'socialism' and 'fascism' for historical supremacy, I find it almost overwhelmingly difficult, knowing what I know, simply to nod sympathetically and pass over in silence the support many Australians gave until quite recently to regimes which systematically murdered and oppressed their populations in pursuit of a dream of social justice. The true believers will impatiently explain, of course, that there was nothing 'socialist' about the Russia I lived in and nothing Marxist about its philosophical underpinnings, but I have to say that it did *feel* as if public ownership of the means of production and distribution along Marxist lines was being experimented with and it felt like a disaster. It felt as if you were on a train that had careered off the rails, grinding countless human lives under its wheels, while the driver sat up in the engine assuring the numb or panic-stricken passengers that everything was under control, everything was going according to plan and here for your edification as the train lurched onto its side were a few more quotations from Karl Marx. This colours your attitude to Karl Marx. It also colours, I hope understandably, your attitude towards the leftist intelligentsia at home who, whatever they may say now, for over half a century declared that you'd either been hallucinating all along (the train had never left the rails) or had never understood why it was *necessary* for revolutionary trains to leave the rails for a brief period. In either case, regardless of the truth, you were supporting the wrong side in their binary construction of the world. You must be 'right-wing', you must be 'conservative', 'reactionary'. Leftism came to mean to me the right to oppress, deceive, lie, kill, wage war, imprison and enslave in the name of an entity called 'the people'. Rightism seemed to be the same thing in the name of an entity called 'the nation'. How these two mystical entities were defined seemed to depend on where your interests lay. But one thing is still clear: past support for the butchers in the Kremlin is not shameful—indeed, it's often construed as a personal tragedy, deserving of sympathy—whereas support for non-socialist butchers *is* shameful. How can you help being cynical?

I've also come to agree with Vaclav Havel's view that social and political problems are *in the first instance* ethical problems, not the other way around. Perhaps you have to spend a few years in a society with a radically different social structure and ideas about justice, equality, goodness or punishment for the strength of Havel's argument to become apparent. It's an argument that gets short shrift in Australian intellectual circles and you learn to be selective about where you voice it. Sympathy for it certainly distances you from the Marxist interpretation of history.

There were things I liked about Russia, all the same, things I miss in Australia. I liked the sense of a shared culture in which everyone took pride. I liked the drama of Christ and the Inquisitor doing daily battle all around you in various forms: in bus queues, in lectures on Tolstoy, during dinner with friends, even in the press, although that was mainly the domain of the Inquisitor. I liked the nights spent talking about important things, about *ideas*, around kitchen tables. Russians know how to converse in a way we don't. Here conversation so often means intersecting monologues, while there it seems to take on a life of its own, it fans out, snaps shut, dips and dives and displays itself. In Russia it's a god-bothering art (and I don't mean in just a religious sense) in many genres, it's not a prelude to any-thing, or just a way of passing the time, or a polite accom-paniment to a meal. It's a time for self-revelation, gossip, passion, argument, negotiation, mockery, sometimes even cruelty. People would drift in and out of the kitchen during the evening—neighbours, friends, enemies, grand-mothers, children, the inhabitants of locked rooms up the corridor—the telephone would ring, the doorbell would buzz, plates of herring or tomatoes or buckwheat would appear on the table, teacups would be filled, long, scan-dalous stories would be told, and then in the early hours of the morning you'd have to go outside onto one of the dark, deserted streets and try to hail a cab to go home (almost no one then had a private car and taxis could not be booked without a two-hour wait). I loved it. It was uncompetitive. There were never just two sides.

Sometimes—just sometimes—in those steamy Moscow kitchens I would wish I was Russian, wish I had that rich, complex culture embedded in me, wish I could swim about inside the Russian language with the same ease my friends could, wish I could let reason and emotion play freely together the way Russians can—but it was a pipe-dream.

I'm deeply un-Russian, despite all those years—most of my life!—spent immersed in things Russian. The desiring, though, was good.

❖ ❖ ❖

There's a superficially boring painting in the National Gallery in London called 'Conversation Piece at the Royal Lodge, Windsor, 1950' by Sir James Gunn. King George, a royal corgi just behind his chair, is having afternoon tea with his wife and daughters, all simply dressed, at an oval table covered in a white damask table-cloth with a lace border drooping almost to the carpet. There's an elegant white marble fireplace at their back with a couple of Chinese vases on it and a gold clock, but really, apart from the height of the room—the chandelier, the gold-framed portrait high up on the blue panelled walls —it could almost be a picture of afternoon tea *en famille* in any upper middle-class home anywhere in the 'fifties. I suspect it's meant to be. It caught my eye because it seemed to me to express an ideal of seemliness, good taste and *bienséance* many aspired to on Sydney's lower North Shore in the 1950s. It's stuffy, of course, placing as it does the man and his dog over and against the idle women—his wife is just fiddling with the tea things—and it promotes the illusion that while the world outside may be a dangerous place where men all too often have to do manly things, they can always find comfort and peace at home in the bosom of the well-dressed family. It demonstrates beautifully why virtue is so important:

without it a man can have no confidence in the value of what he's out in the dangerous world fighting for.

According to the conventional wisdom, this British ideal of family life was widespread in Australia in the 1950s. Australia, so we're told, was a stuffy, sexist, repressed, puritanical society, with not an outdoor café in sight. We were loyal to the Queen and thought of Britain as home. So we're told. It doesn't ring completely true. I never thought of Britain as home and, frankly, don't think I ever knew anyone who did. And although I'm sure Australia was a stuffy, sexist, oppressive, puritanical place for many, I didn't experience it as such. This still makes me feel obscurely guilty. Despite the hysterical anti-Communism in our media, neither my parents nor anyone else ever voiced a word of objection to my growing interest in Russia and the Russian language, while at school I was encouraged to drop Ancient History and study Russian privately in its place. Nor did I experience any objection to my drift into sectarianism. Privately, I'm sure, neighbours and friends felt contempt and surprise, but no one ever stood in my way. Jean and Tom seemed to find my interests eccentric, but not unnatural. I never felt 'marginalised' by being different. Ideological oppression was something I really only came face to face with in the 1980s and 1990s and it came as a shock.

When I was at school in the dreary 1950s, for example, I had no trouble at all being multicultural. In class we studied American, Chinese, Japanese, German and Russian history, we read about the civilisations of ancient Greece and Rome, we learnt Latin, French and German and argued about the political systems and religions of all sorts of societies. After school, in the bookshops in the city, we'd buy paperbacks by Russian novelists, Chinese poets, German philosophers and French existentialists. The country most of us were deeply ignorant about was Australia. I studied no Australian history at school and only one Australian novel that I can remember (*The Passage*, I think it was, by Vance Palmer—all I can remember of it is something about jumping mullet).

It was only thirty years later that I experienced a violent reaction from those who, having built powerful careers on a different kind of multiculturalism, saw my kind of unoppressed multiculturalism as threatening. It was only as a middle-aged man that I began to feel stifled by a kind of post-Marxist philistinism blanketing the fields I was working in. You can catch its characteristic sound sometimes on Radio National—a wearying blend of whining and gloating, oddly reminiscent of student newspapers. I was naïve in the 'fifties and early 'sixties and thought you could be curious about anything—Enid Blyton, masturbation, Marxism—no one seemed to mind. Of course, what I thought as a child didn't matter. I was of no consequence—indeed, we were of no consequence—and there's a certain freedom of the spirit in that.

The Dessaixs, meanwhile, although unbeknownst to me, always thought they *were* of consequence. Blood, *le général*, good stock. There were certain proprieties. So from the day I was

Grandmother, 1938.

Yvonne, 1942.

Strathfield, February 1944.

Baby Jones.

Jean.

Jean and Tom in Austin Street. Pleased to have me.

Tom and I out on the town.

Auntie Eva and Jean, early 'fifties.

The house in Austin Street, Lane Cove.

The sensitive teenager.

Moscow University Pass.

*The Pakistani look. At the ballet with capitalist friends,
the Kremlin, 1967.*

Moscow State University. My Moscow address 1966-7, 1970-1.

Gerringong, 1970.

Elizabeth on the hotel balcony, Wellington, 1977.

Paddington, Sydney, 1980.

Paddington again.

Yvonne at home in western Sydney, 1990.

Gare du Nord, Paris, 1992.

The Brandenburg Gate revisited, 1992.

A red herring, Riom, France, 1992.

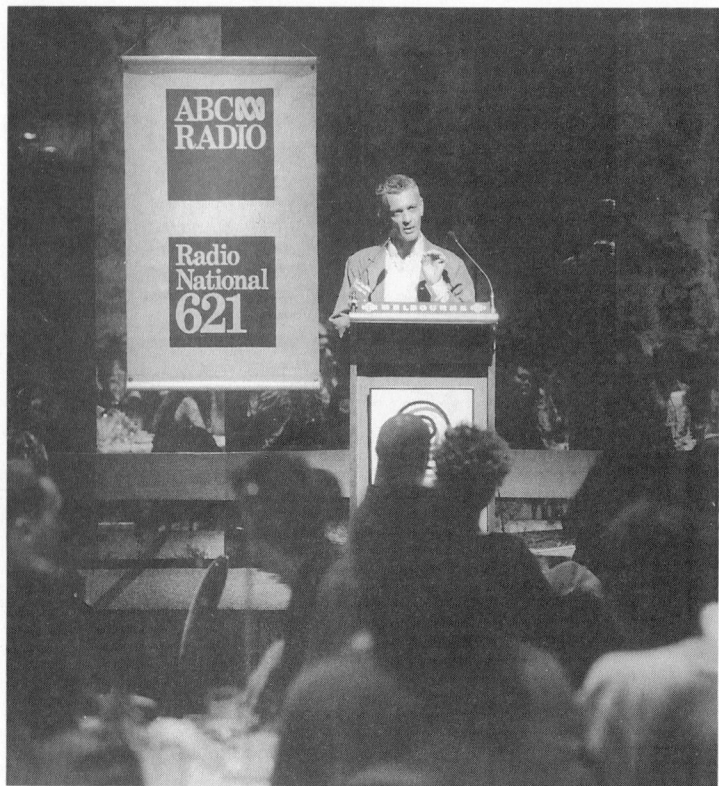

Introducing Armistead Maupin,
Melbourne Hilton, 1993.
(PHOTO COURTESY OF GREG NOAKES)

born, in February 1944, until the day in 1990 Yvonne told her mother she had met me, my embarrassing existence was never referred to. For forty-six years the subject of my existence was never once raised. Yvonne remembers no family visits while she was in the hospital where she'd given birth to me, nor in the home for unmarried mothers in Strathfield where she was put until I was taken from her without a word being spoken, nor back home in the deceptively accommodating bosom of the family, nor in the years that followed, ever, under any circumstances. After that April night in Cairo, a pivotal night—a startlingly mortal night, if I'm honest—while knowing nothing of this silence, I began to plot ways to break into it—not hurriedly, not with any sense of urgency, although there was a moment of breathless panic when I first crossed paths with Yvonne-not-my-mother. It wasn't a matter of rationally devising strategies for finding my mother, but more a matter of alertly desiring something to happen and letting the desire give a shape to my experience. Does that sound tediously abstract? It wasn't, but it did take a little time and a good, sharp jolt.

CHAPTER FOUR

Mother

I'm an aesthete at heart. I try to approach life kaleidoscopically, in sharp bursts. Every now and again I like to give the magic tube a good rattle, hoping fresh circles of colour will flower in the darkness at the other end. It doesn't always work, but it's become a habit. Living life as if it were a fuse you were burning up inch by inch seems wrong-headed to me somehow, but tempting at times, all the same. There's something deeply comforting, after all, about the promise of a linear narrative: birth, school, university, marriage, family, career, onwards, upwards ... the autumnal years a bit misty, perhaps, the phut as the fuse runs out best not thought about too graphically, but on the whole not a bad way to live out a sequence of years. The trouble is that, once you've set out on that alluringly straight track, it's hard to swerve off it or come to a standstill. It's hard to live what I'd call swoopingly.

I have tried to swoop and veer. I didn't have the wit to veer away from marriage, I had to be sent packing. But I did curve away from teaching Russian to university students into working at the Stables Theatre in Kings Cross and then in radio, I did swerve sharply away from Canberra to experiment with being a Sydneysider again, I did deviate (after a messy start) from the heterosexual straight and narrow to try more fulfilling, multifaceted ways of loving, and eventually, in August 1989, à propos of virtually nothing at all, I packed my bags and, leaving Peter and dog to sell the Sydney house and follow later, flew to Melbourne on a one-way ticket. This was just the jolt I'd needed.

The inner northern suburbs of Melbourne are enough to give anyone pause, let alone someone from the hill in Manly. Especially in August. I would pick my way each morning in the drizzle through puddles to the station, graffiti emblazoning every surface, then rattle through what looked to me like a Third World slum—boarded-up shops, grimy factories, bleak little weatherboard bungalows subsiding into their damp gardens amongst lopsided sheds and wrecked cars—to the City, all of which seemed to be the wrong end of somewhere. Perhaps it was being in this kind of no man's land, detached and unencumbered by routines, that brought Yvonne more clearly into focus. Perhaps it was the warm company of my lesbian friends—have you noticed how brimful with enthusiasm many lesbians are for anything to do with motherhood, children, crèches, families, injustice? Perhaps it was the cold and the silence in the evenings there—if there was nothing on SBS, you were forced to curl up somewhere warm and go inside yourself, lesbians always being out of an evening organising something, putting on a play, learning Italian and so on, which is one reason the answering-machine is the central fact of many lesbians' lives (in my experience). Whatever the immediate reason, it was not unhappiness—I'd never have taken the step I next took if I'd been unhappy.

One night after work I decided to do something about Yvonne. I decided to write to the false Yvonne I'd met the previous year, Yvonne-not-my-mother, and lay my cards on the table. It's true she'd said she didn't know another Yvonne, and I'd told her lies about who I was, but writing to her seemed the only practical step to take. So I wrote a very carefully worded letter. I'd copy it out here for you if I'd kept a draft of it, but I didn't—there was nothing in it you ought not read. First of all I admitted to having fudged the truth (as I put it—no one likes to call himself a liar) but said I hoped she'd understand it seemed the wisest thing to do under the circumstances, which I then briefly explained ... illegitimate, Yvonne Dessaix, 1944.

I then made a point which was important to establish right from the start: I said I didn't want anything from my mother, I was content with my life and indeed would not have contacted her if I had not been content with it. I simply wanted to talk with her if she'd like to talk with me. This was absolutely true. I'd always been aware of the danger of meeting my mother at a time of need, a time of loneliness in particular, and there had been quite a few such times over the years. There were days after my marriage broke up when I would become catatonic with loneliness and sit staring at the carpet or the grate in the fireplace for four or five hours until I began to hallucinate. Or I might walk up and down the hallway screaming and banging my fists on the walls. It was tempting at such times to look for Mother.

But now I felt more or less stable, more or less content, and definitely in no need of another mother. In fact, I'd probably had an unnatural number of mothers for one man as it was. Jean had been a loving if over-anxious mother and the leave-taking, as she died, had been agonising. Then there was my mother-in-law whom I still called Mum, and, now she was a widow and could express her feelings more freely, there was Peter's mother as well. And there were all those older women who'd shown what I might call a critical care over the years: Madam Z, Mrs Prokofiev, and a close friend in Canberra, Kate North, who mothered me only in the sense that she treated me with the same mixture of loving kindness and loyal disrespect she did her numerous children. She managed to make you feel special and no better than you should be at the same time.

I was quite pleased with the letter. It was brief, frank and friendly. It was only when I'd finished it I realised I couldn't remember Yvonne's surname or address. I tiptoed through the alphabet in my head until M started flashing, then held my breath as my mind slid down the list: Ma ..., Me ..., Mi ... and then I had it. Not too many of those in Longueville. In a day or two Yvonne M. had my letter.

Finding my mother took her half an hour. A diplomatic phone-call to this family member or that, some harmless concoction about needing to get in touch, and she had my mother on the line. Now for the hard bit—and Yvonne M.

carried it off with astounding aplomb. She said she had met me and had reason to believe that she, Yvonne Dessaix-that-was, might be my mother. Then she read her my letter. Yvonne Dessaix-that-was needed a little time to think.

In fact, I now know, she was distraught. 'I went hot and cold, hot and cold,' she told me, 'I couldn't believe it, I just couldn't believe it.' Her mother had just almost died and was still sitting in her chair needing tender care—Yvonne was spending every other week looking after her—and suddenly a name had been spoken which had not been spoken for nearly fifty years, a name that meant anguish.

Wrestling with that anguish but partly reassured, she later told me, by the lines I'd written about not wanting to interfere in her life or ask anything of her, Yvonne picked up the telephone and dialled my number at work. After nearly half a century the silence was about to be broken, but, unfortunately, I was in the toilet and missed the call.

A few days later a letter came, a delicate, considered note on frail paper, not cool but restrained, correct. I could telephone her if I wished. I suppose, to be quite honest, I'd hoped for something just a little more effusive, but I could tell from the wording that this woman had found this letter distressingly difficult to write.

When the time came, I simply didn't feel bold enough to pick the telephone up and start speaking. What do you say? 'Hullo, how are you?' 'Mother, it's me?' Impossible. In the end I asked a friend who'd encouraged me to take this step all along to call her and ask if she'd like to speak to me. And so we spoke. Tentatively, shyly, happily, with me no doubt eventually putting on my slightly over-bright 'do have another cake' sort of voice to carry me through the occasion and Yvonne sounding, as usual, compliant but somehow doughty at the same time. I was very busy analysing her accent, ever the linguist. We agreed I'd go to Sydney and we'd meet.

This sort of thing called for careful choreographing, as you can imagine. You can't just meet on the Town Hall steps at 12.30, after all, or in one of your own homes (too immediately intimate, too territorially fraught), you can't really even meet in a restaurant (too prim, too distracting). So where? We settled on Yvonne M.'s house in Longueville—a benign presence, family but neutral, and as well a certain narrative rightness, as I'm sure you'll agree.

Apart from anything else, this was a house I had walked past hundreds if not thousands of times in my childhood. It was on a route I took on countless late afternoon walks with the dog—clipped lawns and nature strips, luxuriant gardens, the Lane Cove river glinting through the trees to the west, just the kind of quiet, green streets to stroll along with a nosy dog, talking to yourself in foreign languages. The house was also, oddly enough, just around the corner from the Presbyterian church I'd been fruitlessly christened in and led up the garden path in about Jesus. Perhaps not quite fruitlessly.

I arrived outside the house early, I remember, striped shirt all ironed, and had to go off and sit in the nearby park for a while thinking pacifying thoughts. Then I walked back across to the house, greeted Yvonne M. at the backdoor and was told to walk through to the living-room. My mother was waiting for me there alone. What you say, it turns out, is 'Hullo'. Then you kiss and then you just look and smile and want to laugh and laugh and say nothing and everything all at once. There's a kind of tumult you feel at the still centre of. That's all I can say. Now I really want to write just *dot dot dot* and turn away from those two people in that room because the words won't come. I'd like to make a joke or engage your attention (and mine) somewhere else. But I'll try to find the words. Let me start with Yvonne.

As she told me afterwards, there was, of course, a kind of piercing joy, but I came towards her out of a terrible remoteness with the eyes of my father. She felt, I think, almost physically struck down. My eyes—how do you describe your own eyes?—are large and green-hazel. Suddenly, after a lifetime, unhoped-for and unthought-of, my father's eyes were near again, a hand's breadth away. Yvonne said nothing, she just looked and smiled a smile of boundless hurt and happiness.

'I thought you were rather aloof, you know,' she said to me later, when we'd got to know each other better. She underlined 'aloof' exactly the way I would. 'Were you?' What an odd question. I liked it. I said I supposed I had been a bit. Now I've met her mother, I think haughtiness runs in the family, although in Yvonne it's been savagely beaten back to a kind of resigned dignity. 'I didn't think you were unpleasant,' she added, 'in fact, I thought you were lovely.' (I apologise for writing that, but it *is* what she later said.) 'But aloof.'

After a while we went out onto the balcony under the overhanging trees with views over to the college Aunty Eva had wanted to send me to all those years ago (the same college Yvonne M.'s sons went to) and across houses and streets I'd known and belonged to throughout my childhood. Yet in front of me, across the wooden table, framed by those streets and houses and waterscapes, was the mother who had always just been a story in my head. And so we began to ask each other questions, like friends of friends, in a way, discovering each other on a train journey.

'Are you married, Robert?' she asked me, looking hopeful. I hate that question. 'No, I'm not,' I said, and I knew Yvonne could see grandchildren going up in smoke. 'But I was once,' I said, and I knew she could see them taking wispy form again. 'But we had no children,' I said, perhaps a little too forcefully. Up in smoke again. 'Do you think you might get married again one day?' 'No, I don't think so.' A pause now I was clearly expected to fill in. 'I think,' I said—let's not rush this—'I'm moving in a different direction.' 'Ah,' said Yvonne, disappointed but none the wiser. I went on to explain I lived with a friend called Peter and had done for quite a few years, although I was staying at the moment in Melbourne with two lesbian friends. ('You're *not*!' she cried, aghast.) I thought I'd dropped enough clues for anyone to pick up, but I was wrong. I thought: 'Skip it.'

Yvonne sketched in her life—her two sons, two husbands,

her life now looking after Mother—alluded to the fine stock I came from, asked about Jean and Tom and whether life had worked out well for me (but could see it had), and then said: 'You know, I thought you'd feel bitter.' Bitter? This was unexpected. I had no idea what she might mean. Why would I feel bitter? 'I thought you might feel I'd abandoned you, I thought you might say, Look, why did you give me away? I thought: what if you don't like me?' She looked so tiny then, like a little sparrow.

I didn't feel bitter, bitterness was beside the point, apart from the fact that I now knew Yvonne was in my terms (not hers) blameless. Yet, curiously enough, she'd hit on a root word in my shaky construction of myself, the very word a few years before a psychiatrist had made use of over and over again until it had lost its power: abandoned. And it was true, the word was subtly linked with the day at the unmarried mothers' home in Strathfield when my mother had 'let me go', and with the mysterious story Tom had told me when I was very small—how could he possibly have known? he swore he didn't know my father's name—about my father dying in an air-crash, abandoning me doubly. And then with all the other abandonings and deaths and castings-off, until the day in the psychiatrist's room (only the fourth visit, I hasten to add) when the word had exploded into three syllables signifying nothing.

I did ask Yvonne a little about my father on that first day. I was curious, but there was little she could tell me or felt moved to tell me quite so soon. He was no Hungarian count, however, that much was clear. Nor, in case Aunty Moat is peering at these lines through her bifocals, was he an Aborigine.

We spent several hours together out on Yvonne M.'s balcony in the sun, talking. As we parted, I felt a rush of affection, of thankfulness to this woman for being what she was, of completeness at last—no, not completeness, but completion, of weaving two parts together to make a whole. You must think me a dry old stick not to speak of love and joy and souls united. I'm sorry. Tumult, yes, but love and joy and the uniting of souls do not burst from the sky, at least, in my experience, for the child. We started, speaking at least for myself, with affection and—this may also sound cold to you, but it wasn't—avid attention. We started, in other words, with deep, generous liking and thankfulness that the silence had been broken.

❖ ❖ ❖

In all those years someone must surely have said something. The silence cannot have been absolute. One of Yvonne's sisters, perhaps, at a sentimental moment, to another of her sisters, if not to their formidable mother, a handsome woman, hair combed tightly back, who dominates every family photograph I've seen by simply being there. (She has that slightly arrogant 'Oh, really?' look I have myself and when we eventually met she looked at me and said: 'You are mine.' A little late in the day, I might say.)

Actually, someone has said something. A sister has rung Yvonne and sent her a photograph. Quite out of the blue. I'm looking at it now. It's in a small folder with Paxton's Prints written on it (black and white ninepence, sepia one shilling). It's a tiny, square photograph and it moves me deeply. My mother Yvonne is sitting on a bench in a garden at the girls' home near Strathfield where we were taken from the hospital, holding me low in her arms. I am about to be taken from her. She knows this, but doesn't know when. She's looking at the camera with an expression of grave resignation and wounded wisdom, as if she'd just watched a ship sail away forever with someone on it she loved. I, of course, am lying back enjoying the sun.

Yvonne has no memory of any photograph being taken, or, for that matter, of any visitors at all. When the photograph arrived in the mail from her sister she was very distressed. She showed it to me a few days later in a café in Kings Cross and we both just sat in silence for about five minutes staring at it. When I looked up I caught just an echo of the bitter dignity of the photograph on Yvonne's small-boned face. But we mustn't grow maudlin—the fish is sweet, we're enjoying each other's company in a quiet, undemonstrative sort of way, and so I take another snapshot from Paxton's yellowing folder, this time of grandmama and her seven children, and I start to make jokes about who's the best-looking. Grandmama, of course, has the air of some duchess from Mitteleuropa, completely ruthless with the peasants.

I found she wasn't nearly as fearsome as she looked, by

the way, when I eventually met her. She was seeing no one, being in her mid-nineties and frailer than she'd like to be, but she agreed to see me for afternoon tea. It was like an audience and I flew up from Melbourne specially. I was so yellow at the time with some disease that I couldn't stand in the check-in queue long enough to check in and almost missed the plane, but I knew I had to go. Perhaps she thought I was always yellow. At any rate she gave no sign of minding. When Yvonne ushered me into the dining-room where she was sitting, in the house she'd lived in for over seventy years—the house my mother had grown up in and come home to from Strathfield without me—she greeted me warmly and we recognised each other. It was a strange moment, as you can imagine. Here I was turning up again, almost half a century after she'd given instructions I should be taken away and never spoken of again.

You'd think it would be an occasion for exchanging profundities, wouldn't you, but it wasn't. The profundities were all at the level of feelings, not words. We talked about this and that: her health, how the district had changed (half the population no longer seemed to speak English), about Yvonne in front of her as if she wasn't there—how good she was, what a wonderful daughter ... Of course she was a wonderful daughter—she spent half her life, week about with a brother, living with her mother and looking after her like a district nurse. Yvonne brought out sausage-rolls and cakes and I felt even yellower.

Yes, we recognised each other. I looked at this clear-eyed

matriarch, with her fine skin and knowing smile and mind that missed nothing, and she looked at me, and we knew we belonged. She felt, I'm sure, not a twinge of guilt for what had happened, she seemed serenely confident that she'd simply done what had had to be done. It was a matter of breeding. (She, too, by the way, has French blood. She's a Bullivant and to this day likes to pronounce the name without the 't'. The French pronounce it without the 'n' as well.) She seemed curious and pleased to note I'd turned out, on the whole, rather well, but in no need of intimacy or attachment. When I got into the taxi an hour and a half later, I felt sure she expected the silence to wash back quietly over me again.

Can you imagine what it felt like, going into that dark house with its heavy furniture and family photographs on polished surfaces (photographs pretending I didn't exist), my own mother welcoming me at the front door? It seemed a stern and righteous house to me, a house of good people, a bastion of principles, the sort of house children might be strapped in. Almost as if I'd known, I've grown up with a taste for houses with french windows, skylights, verandahs (back, front, side)—I love the orangerie effect.

It was into this sturdy bungalow, I now know, in Sydney's higgledy-piggledy, dreary mid-west that Yvonne my mother was born. Nowadays it's scarred with tasteless blocks of flats with aluminium window-frames and drive-in fast-food outlets. People have moved in with their own unrelated histories and little interest in what was there before. There are mosques on the horizon. But when Yvonne was born in the mid-twenties, Campsie was still a red-roofed middle-class suburb at the edge of the city sprawl, there were even paddocks behind the houses with horses and cows in them, paddocks you could fly kites in. Here Yvonne and her six brothers and sisters went to school (you could see it from the window), here she joined the Music Society, dancing in the chorus-line of the odd Sunday night show—*The Pirates of Penzance*, perhaps, or it might have been *The Maid of the Mountains*. She'd wanted as a girl (she's still petite) to be a ballet dancer and gone to Estelle Anderson's studio in Rowe Street in the city, but, naturally, it had come to nothing. Just a few years later and just a few miles across the city, I wanted to become a dancer, too, as if Yvonne had given up in Campsie and passed the desire on to me in Lane Cove. I'd just seen *The Red Shoes* and insisted that Jean and Tom send me to dancing classes. This should have alerted them to the fact that there was something strange about me from the start, but they sent me anyway, Jean, I think, with some misgivings, Tom in his usual spirit of letting me follow my inclinations. My classes didn't lead to anything, either.

It was an idyllic life, Yvonne now thinks, looking back. I asked her very recently what it was *like*, living there, in that house, at that time. 'Well, it was like David Malouf,' she said, to my considerable surprise, I admit. She was thinking, I suppose, of *12 Edmondstone Street*. It must have been a tribal life they led, by my lights, with the sort of tribal pleasures I've never really known, nor for that matter wanted. Still, I shouldn't feel supercilious towards them, to Yvonne they were obviously real enough.

One Melbourne Cup day just before the war, with his bets all written out, Yvonne's father suddenly died. In some ways you might say that's when Yvonne's step faltered, although Yvonne herself would probably not say that. She'd loved her father rather too much—I can tell that even now when she talks about him to me, trying to convey to me his goodness. A fearful thing, goodness of the suburban kind. I have no faith in it, but Yvonne does, having been schooled in it. Her father was an imposing-looking, upright man, with his own leather business in his backyard (the cavernous workshop is still there, hot and musty, a mausoleum). He was religiously inclined, a Mason, and was dead against any noise from the children when they were playing in the front yard. It seems to have been a bit of a family obsession, this horror of noise, of undisciplined speech, of rumour and bruiting abroad. Good music was another matter altogether. He loved his wind-up gramophone.

Yvonne was grief-stricken when her father died. Some pillar had crumbled, not to be replaced. In her anguish she refused to go back to school. 'Mother hit the roof.' I can imagine. Mother still hits the roof and she's nearly a hundred. A severely beautiful woman (overshadowingly beautiful, Yvonne says)—just a touch of lipstick when she stepped out in one of her ballgowns from the Strand Arcade and the merest hint of vaseline on eyebrows and eyelashes—her wrath must have been impressive. But Yvonne could be stubborn too ('cheeky', she calls it), slight though she was and only fifth in line. She did not go back to school, she went to business college for a year and did, as she puts it, very well. Needless to say, there was no question of a university education in those good old pre-war days, a right Yvonne's grandchildren take for granted. The Dessaixs were what was called 'comfortably off': the children ate well (although only the older children could have an apple each), were properly clothed, wore shoes and lived in a solid house with a neat front garden and beds of potatoes, rhubarb, peas and tomatoes out the back. This was more than could be said for all the children in the district, some of whom walked to school in cracked bare feet. Yet apparently none of Yvonne's family aspired to a university education.

With the older boys away at the war, Yvonne began to live the kind of life I suppose many middle-class young women were leading. She went to work as a secretary at Verey's, a tailoring business in King Street in the city. Verey's had a military contract and young servicemen would drop in to have wings or stripes sewn on or some adjustment made to their uniform. At sixteen years of age, beautiful in quite a dusky, Mediterranean sort of way, Yvonne was engaged to be married to a young man we might call Gordon who worked with her at Verey's. Gordon gave her a ring he'd bought at Saunders the jewellers one Friday night. Mother hit the roof again, Yvonne tried to pull the ring off her finger and couldn't get it off, Gordon's mother hit the roof ...

but the war was on and allowances seem to have been made. Gordon was soon sent to New Guinea, leaving Yvonne to her duties at Verey's and at home. It's a familiar story, but with a twist—myself.

Now, Yvonne, as she recalls it, led a relatively carefree life during the war. Or at least a blameless life, according to the mores of the tribe. She might go on a ferry-ride to Manly with a young man or group of friends, or sit in a city park with sandwiches, she might go ice-skating or play tennis or go to a live show at a theatre like the Minerva in Kings Cross (we both love a good show) with the girls from the office. A couple of men on leave might join them. Much scurrying about with shampoos, lipstick, shoe-polish. Kings Cross, just a mile or so away from Verey's on a ridge to the east, was seething with God knows what during the war, but none of it seems to have touched Yvonne: the raucous world of winebars, sly grog shops, *maisons de passe* and illicit pleasures of an even more outlandish kind—Yvonne seems hardly to have been aware it was there. It simply did not lure her, as it might have lured me. Fifty years later, when we met at Kings Cross station to walk to a café and chat, I said to her, waving an arm at the soaring hotel towers and the mess of underpasses and over-passes: 'It's probably changed a lot since you were last here.' 'Well, yes, it has,' she said, looking at me rather than at Kings Cross. 'When were you here last?' I said (conversation doesn't always flow just because you're related). 'In 1943,' she said, unaware this was unusual. She's lived in and around the city all her life.

On weekends Yvonne would go horse-riding with friends in the bush north of the city. Occasionally they might camp overnight, but there was no thought of any Goings On, she assures me. Literally no thought. If some of the older members of the group took advantage of the situation, Yvonne was protected from knowing about it. She tells me that as a six-teen- or seventeen-year-old girl from a good background, she had no sexual knowledge, or sense of lack of knowledge, at all. Not even curiosity. Curiosity, after all, has to be fed. Sex, she tells me, was not spoken of at home, at work or on outings. 'You see, Robert,' she said to me once when we talking about those Maloufian days, 'I was a sitting duck.' Masculinity, which she clearly did find desirable, meant something very particular to Yvonne, it now seems. It meant what she calls 'being a gentleman'. It meant being like her brothers. This cannot have been a wholly bad thing. Nor wholly good, of course, which is why I'm awkwardly here to tell this tale.

I am a disgrace, you see. In later years I disgraced *myself* often enough, not unexpectedly, and I disgraced my wife, I think now, by being rather too interested in an unmentionable religion and not quite interested enough in men—she instinctively knew early on that manly men are drawn to men and men's things, not to women, except to woo and bed them. (Many Australian men are simply neutered, afraid to be drawn in any direction. Some of them neuter their wives as well and have a good go at neutering their children. This is *not* a disgrace.) But I was born a disgrace.

Even after we'd met, and Yvonne was telling me about her life both before and after I was born, she said to me, quite unconscious of what she was saying: 'By having you I disgraced the family name.' I was a bit put out. 'Well,' she said, 'it must've been a dreadful shock to Mother ... the war was on and the boys were gone and so forth ... I still feel that sense of guilt ... the disgrace of it has remained.' The remedy for disgrace in that family has been a suffocating blanket of silence. (Not only in that family, needless to say: my affectionate mother-in-law, for some odd reason, likes to refer to me gently with outsiders as her adopted son, as if the truth—that I am her daughter's ex-husband—were somehow too shameful to mention directly. And although I've lived with Peter now for some twelve years, his family, with the exception of his mother and two aunts, simply see a blank space where I am standing. All good people, of course, according to their lights.)

One day in 1943, a day so ordinary my mother can't remember it clearly, an airman on leave dropped into Verey's to have a coloured patch sewn on, got talking to the rather refined-looking manager's secretary (sometimes she'd act as telephonist—it was a small business) and they agreed to meet after work. He may have suggested coffee at Repin's just up the street, if he'd wanted to impress with something Continental, or in a slightly more urbane mood they may have walked across to Rowe Street and had a pot of tea in one of those small places with blue-and-white checked tablecloths and modernist prints on the walls. For a hundred yards or so in Rowe Street, amongst the shops displaying craft objects, the tea-rooms with pots of geraniums on the window-sill and signs beside doorways reading: *Drama Society: up two flights*, you could almost be in England.

Style was all very well (what could be had of it), but Yvonne liked to get home to the family pretty promptly after work, so in all probability Yvonne and Harry (that seems to have been the nice-looking young pilot's name) walked the few blocks down to Wynyard Station. By this time she'd become more or less disengaged from Gordon, they were too alike, they'd decided, so it wasn't likely to work. A remarkably mature viewpoint to take at just eighteen. I was twice that age before I came to understand it.

The ramp leading down into the bowels of Wynyard Station was lined, as it is today, with an assortment of shops and kiosks selling everything from shoelaces to magazines and ice-creams. For a tentative first step in a courtship it was perfect, if lacking in class. What could be more innocent than a chocolate milkshake on Wynyard ramp on the way to catch your train? Escape was so easy, offence lightly avoided. Or so it must have seemed at the time.

What exactly happened next seems rather unclear, and although I'm by no means uninterested, it's not really something I can ask about. 'I went out with him quite a lot,' Yvonne says, 'with friends. He was a very nice chap.' There doesn't seem to have been any grand passion—why should there have been? it's not obligatory—but there was enough strong feeling for a certain mark to be overstepped on one occasion. Unfortunately (if I might again speak of myself as a misfortune), that was enough to change for good the course of Yvonne's life. It still seems to me that the disarray, if I can put it that way, that resulted from meeting Harry has never quite resolved itself.

To this day, when she speaks of that time, she speaks of having done something immoral. To tell the absolute truth, I find this confusing and painful and wish she wouldn't say it. The first time she said it I could feel tears in the back of my throat. I said something brightly modern back, I remember, and then we both fell quiet.

Falling pregnant, as Yvonne might put it, came as a shock to her. From what I can gather, she really does not seem to have made a strong connection between what had happened with Harry and pregnancy. As if it were some unspeakable disease only the poor were prone to, no one in the family appears to have thought it proper to point the connection out. Some months after meeting my father, Yvonne had left Verey's and was stationed as a typist at Clifton Gardens. Feeling exhausted in a way she knew was 'not quite right', but putting it down to the long route marches she'd been on, Yvonne took herself to Victoria Barracks for an examination. She was shocked and dismayed to be told she was pregnant. 'I promptly fell in a heap,' she said.

She was called up to the adjutant and 'drummed out of the army', as she puts it. 'They didn't have single girls' pensions or things like that in those days. I had nowhere to go but Mother's.' One other possibility did unexpectedly present itself, she now recalls, and that was a proposal to marry her (regardless, I take it) from the adjutant's aide at Clifton Gardens. (Oddly enough, he had the same unusual name and came from the same suburb as the woman I first asked to take me to church. Was it her son? Was there a cosmic plot to have me live in Austin Street, Lane Cove, come what may?) Another fork in the road, but she didn't take that turning and I think it's only now, fifty years later, she realises it was a real option. But Yvonne is not wistful by nature.

So she went home to Mother's and was 'hidden from sight', as she says. Mother, as we know, was deeply shocked. Yvonne had the freedom of the house—only her sisters and younger brother were at home—but had to go to her room if anyone called. Only at night, under cover of darkness, could she leave the house. The next-door neighbours, she remembers specifically, were not to know anything. There was no discussion of the situation. 'Neither then nor since,' she says now. 'It's never been mentioned.'

As soon as she knew she was pregnant, she telephoned Harry, who was still in Australia. He didn't believe it. He said he'd ring back later, but he didn't. In fact, he left for the war the next day and for security reasons it was impossible to find out where he'd been sent. Yvonne and Harry never met or spoke again. And then he was dead. Not that anyone thought to tell her. She came across it in the evening newspaper a couple of years later. A helicopter had crashed. There was even a photograph—the only one, incidentally, she ever had. Not that she could cut it out and keep it, that would not have been quite right, Yvonne says, under the circumstances. The circumstances were that she was now married to Gordon with another child. A legitimate one. All above board.

Yvonne actually missed another fork in the road. Well, she less missed it than was led blindfolded past it by Mother. My father did return on leave to Sydney and did telephone, but the call was taken by Mother. He wanted to speak to Yvonne but Mother would not hear of it. It took Mother fifty years or so to mention this telephone call to Yvonne. It took, in fact, my reappearance on the scene. 'I was really livid,' Yvonne told me. But she has forgiven Mother, whom she sees as someone who has always done what she thought was best. A terrible thing to say about anyone in my book, but life has taught the two of us very different lessons. 'If only she'd let me speak to him that day, you might've had a father,' she said to me. 'A proper father.' 'I did have a proper father,' I said. 'Yes, of course you did,' she said, 'I don't mean to be disrespectful.' And I caught myself wishing she had been more disrespectful all along.

In February 1944 Yvonne was taken to a dungeon in Crown Street, hardly a mile from where she'd first met Harry, for the climax of this thoroughly disgraceful affair. She understood that the decision had been made that her baby was to be adopted. The decision had been made, needless to say, by Mother. No one in those days appears to have thought of consulting with the mother. Yvonne was, after all, totally dependent on her mother economically—'Mother must even have paid the hospital bill', Yvonne says, even now not ungratefully—so she took it for granted that she was without a voice on the subject of her future. Some sort of murky business went on at Crown Street hospital well out of Yvonne's sight and hearing. I know (as Yvonne did not until I told her) that Jean and Tom inspected me in my bassinet at the hospital and were taken with the way I fixed my crossed eyes on them and roared, and I also know (as Yvonne did not) that the almoner at the hospital met my father, Harry. She gave Jean and Tom a report on him which they passed on to me. So I can only presume he came to the hospital and sat talking to the almoner yards away from the woman who had had his child on the understanding that he would not try to see her or speak to her. With whom did he have this understanding? With Mother? My mother remembers to this day feeling 'a strong dislike' for the almoner, but it's a guilty memory because, as she says of her antipathy, 'it must have made Mother feel dreadful.' These are lines of guilt and blame so insidious, so intricate, someone of my generation can barely disentangle them.

Yvonne remembers no visitors at all, either at the hospital or at the home for unmarried mothers near Strathfield she was taken to shortly after the birth. The photograph (not fading at all, it's very sharp) proves that at least one sister visited her. And one day, shortly after it was taken, I was gone. Yvonne knew I was to be taken from her, but not when. One day I was just not there any more. She didn't say goodbye. I vanished and the matter was not spoken of again.

'Did you have a sense of grief?' I asked her, when I knew her better.

'Well, yes, I did,' she said.

'And did it last a long time?'

'Well, yes, it did, Robert. It just never goes away, actually.'

Yvonne was feeling rather 'annoyed' with Harry, as she now says, characteristically using a word that underlines her lack of any right to a more powerful, self-assertive emotion. If the truth be known, I think she was almost maddened with grief. She thought he'd tried to 'cut her out of his life' and was allowed to keep thinking this for almost fifty years. So she was inclined to let him fade. To this day she seems unsure of his background, who his parents were, exactly where he came from, whether he had any brothers or sisters—the sort of thing memory usually records very sharply when we're in love or even just rather smitten. To this day she seems curiously detached from any clear memory of my father, except for the eyes, although I may be misjudging her. At any rate, the lack of interest is catching.

When Gordon came back from New Guinea shortly before my birth, he and Yvonne became engaged again and married the month after I was born. And had a strikingly good-looking son. I've only seen photographs of him—he's dead now, like Harry and also Gordon. They make me smile because, whereas I can see little of myself in my mother, I can see quite a lot of myself in the half-brother I never met and shared nothing with. The way he stands, the knees, the angle of the head, the expression. And here I was thinking I was self-made.

Over the half-century since March 1944 the gap between the paths our lives have taken has yawned wider and wider. You can imagine, when I did eventually one day walk into that room in Longueville and kiss my mother on the cheek, what care we had to exercise to begin bridging that gap without falling into it.

Some things we shared. Neither of us, for example, had proved much good at marriage while expecting a lot from it. Her marriage to Gordon, at least as she relates it now, seems to have turned into something akin to a musical comedy: Yvonne would live with Gordon for a week, decide the whole thing was impossible and go back to Mother's with their child. Poor Mother, she says. It was really only when they started getting divorced that things picked up: he'd call in to Mother's, they'd go out dancing or to the cinema, spend an enjoyable evening together and then he'd drop her back at Mother's. The ending was not comic: Gordon had had a bad time in New Guinea, suffered serious mental disturbance and died in his late thirties. 'So were they unhappy years?' I asked Yvonne, meaning no more than to prompt her to describe the precise kind of unhappiness she'd experienced. 'Oh, no, not at all,' she said, 'Gordon and I were very good friends.'

What a deeply puzzling word 'friend' is. I don't understand it, yet I sometimes feel if I did many things would become clearer. This shifty English monosyllable covers such a vast and amorphous mass of emotions, loyalties, attachments and feelings that you can never be sure exactly what anyone

115

means when they use it. Whatever it is, sex doesn't seem to go together with it very well, historically speaking, perhaps because sex seems to involve masked power-games and in friendship the illusion of equality is at least fostered. Obviously a sexual relationship can be coloured with all sorts of feelings proper to friendship, but I don't think it's common for people to want to have sex with the people they call their friends. Yet for some reason I don't fully understand men and women are supposed either to invest their permanent sexual relationship with that vast range of emotions and loyalties we call 'friendship' or else they're expected to choose one member of the opposite sex they consider a 'friend' and invest the friendship with a symphonic range of sexual feelings. *En exclusivité.* This seems to me to be a tragically impoverishing arrangement for all concerned. Gordon was obviously a friend, not a husband. Dovetailing the two might work, but why try to conflate them down to the last millimetre? (Basically, I suppose, because it turns us into neatly squared-off building blocks to build a neatly squared-off, vertically stable society out of. No lop-sided hexagons, fish-shapes or rubber-boot-shapes allowed, except at the top, where they won't rock the boat.)

For over ten years in the late 'forties and early 'fifties, Yvonne lived mostly at Mother's, making leathergoods in the factory her father had built and Mother still ran at the back of the house in Campsie. Unwisely (in my view) she then opted for a husband rather than a friend. I don't think she'd put it like that, and might even object strongly to my putting it like that, but, as she tells the story, it becomes clear that by her early thirties she was (how should I phrase it?) deeply disappointed in men; except for her brothers, who seem to have retained for her a kind of pre-war gentlemanly glow. I don't know them—and am sure they would not want to know me—so can't comment. But Yvonne is sure that men were different before the war. She's mentioned this to me several times. I don't think she means simply that sexual mores were different, but that 'a good man' meant something different, something more reassuring, kindly and reliable. 'I thought they were a dreadful lot,' she said to me once, meaning post-war men, 'real villains.' All the same, she eventually married a man we might call Colin, a much older, well-travelled, knowledgeable man she'd met through her brothers—a husband. When she described him in those words to me, I couldn't help smiling. 'Oh, yes,' she said, smiling the same kind of smile, 'I know what you're thinking. You're thinking of what the psychologists would say, aren't you?'

Yvonne is a tiny woman, you'd think she'd blow away, and when she first sat and told me about the years that followed (over twenty) she seemed to shrivel up into something even tinier before my eyes, something about to be trodden on and crushed. In a sense I was wrong, my perspective was skewed, it wasn't all grinding misery, but as I listened to my mother speak about those years I could feel my breathing slow to almost nothing. For a while she worked for no wage in Colin's shop, hardly any distance at all from

Mother's. They lived above it. Her reward (perhaps from Colin's point of view a practical arrangement, we have no right to judge him harshly) was to be a holiday in Noumea (the French connection) and, eventually, 'a lovely home'. Middle-class dreams, you may be thinking, but scarcely greedy ones. In fact, there was no 'lovely home' and no trip to Noumea. To this day she's hardly been more than a hundred miles from home, except to attend her son's funeral. That was two hundred miles away.

She had another child and, in the late 'sixties, Yvonne, Colin and the two boys moved to a beautiful part of the coast north of Sydney, an area of estuaries and bushland and bright yellow beaches with holiday shacks dotted up the hillsides behind them. For some years Yvonne worked picking tomatoes and beans on a nearby farm. Eventually an RSL club opened in the growing township and she walked over to see if it might have a job for her. It did, as a cleaner. 'I was greatly surprised,' she told me, as if still not wholly able to believe in her good fortune. 'It was good, honest work.' And went on for many years.

It was a township Yvonne and her family had spent holidays in several times before they moved there, and, strange to relate, during those same years I spent two summer holidays there myself as a child. There was only one road to speak of in those days, running up the hill from the ocean beach, across the bushy ridge and down again to the ferry-wharf on Brisbane Water, all oyster leases and warm, briny air heavy with eucalyptus. That's where the shop was, down opposite the wharf. We no doubt passed each other on the road sometimes, going in and out of our separate houses, waited behind each other in the shop, perhaps, or even climbed onto the little ferry together to go into Woy Woy. I probably saw my half-brothers pottering around the rocks on the ocean side like me, poking their fingers into sea-anemones or catching crabs in bottles. But it wasn't a movie—it was real life and nothing happened.

While Yvonne was working in that shop in Campsie and picking tomatoes and cleaning up after the local returned servicemen in that settlement by the sea, I was living a very different life, as you'll have gathered, mostly at the university in Canberra. For a teenager whose father was a mere messenger-boy (he'd come out of retirement to take on this job) and mother a part-time baby health centre sister, the ANU was a shimmering foreign land, seething with conflicting certainties. Canberra even turned a fiery red in late April like real European cities and in August it might occasionally snow. Important people popped up everywhere: A. D. Hope might say a word to you in the library, Manning Clark might take a tutorial, the Prime Minister's wife was in our French class and one of the Whitlam boys was living in college. It was like a vast live-in club for the intelligentsia and everyone seemed to be moving onwards and upwards into university posts, the diplomatic corps, jobs in America. People took holidays in England and Italy—even the students—and seemed to take it for granted that they had a valued contribution to make to something or other. Writing, talking, arguing, analysing, reading—we were born to it.

Up to a point, of course, it was stressful coming face to face with a world which fundamentally disagreed with you about absolutely everything—disagreed and patronised. If you're a Hindu in Budapest, you at least have the protection of your cultural cocoon, woven over millennia, but I had no cocoon: my culture was basically everyone else's culture, only my ideas were different. Lunatic, some must have said. I coped, as I do now, mainly by treating all the world-views we were served up as tales that were told, to be understood on their own terms, as you might study the Koran and even become learned in it—or *A Brief History of Time* or Derrida, for that matter—without either espousing or rejecting the doctrines you're encountering. It was like studying the street-maps of cities you never expected to visit. Deep down convictions brew—how could they not?—a core attitude hardens, dissolves, reforms, but I'm beginning to suspect, now I've met my mother and grandmother, that more of what forms deep down is innate than I once thought, less open to remoulding by the purveyors of advanced new social doctrines than I'd hoped.

By the late 'eighties both Yvonne and I, each unaware of the other, had resettled in Sydney to contemplate starting new lives after our marriages had broken up miserably. (Not that Yvonne blames anyone for her unhappiness: 'The trouble I've been in I've brought upon myself,' she told me firmly once, lest I imagine she held anyone else to blame.) It would be nice to think we passed each other on the steps at Town Hall Station or walking up George Street, but we probably didn't. Yvonne was living on the western outskirts of the city, a long train ride from Mother's, in what once would have been called severely reduced circumstances, while Sydney for me meant a Paddington terrace, the fringes of the theatre world, dinner in Oxford Street cafés, and latterly a large house on the hill at Manly, bays and bushy headland glimpsed through banana palms, gums and towering cordylines. Yet I was beginning to think of her now, not melodramatically as I might once have done at some agonising adolescent moment, or hopefully or needfully, but, after that night in Cairo, mainly because I felt I wanted depth to my story, some sort of verticality I could run up and down in my mind, not just breadth—I'd had that in abundance. That may sound dry and calculating just when you'd hoped for something heart-felt. In reality it *was* heart-felt, it's just that I'm choosing my words with great care.

And Yvonne, if I've understood her, never stopped thinking about me. One of the most touching things she said to me when eventually we met and sat down and talked for the first time was that every year on my birthday she would try to spend the day alone, unencumbered, if possible, by any distracting duties, and think about me. She said it very gently and simply, as if I must have known. 'But I didn't do it this year,' she said. As if *she* had known.

CHAPTER FIVE

Another
Disgrace

Yvonne's first visit to our house was going well. There'd been a small catastrophe as she arrived—the strap on one of the new white shoes she'd bought for the occasion had snapped as she was coming down our steep front steps. But Peter had manfully mended it. And he'd fried the bream and made the salad while we talked. And now, lunch and easy table conversation over, Yvonne and I were out on the back balcony overlooking the ocean at Manly. It was hot and the conversation was slowing down. You'd think nothing could be simpler, wouldn't you? Two people attached by the strongest bonds there are, two whole lives to recount, so many unexpected stories to tell. Yet it wasn't easy. Conversation grows out of a sense of something shared: an interest in gardening, Sanskrit, friends, anything. We were mother and son but had shared nothing at all. Yvonne hadn't even known my name. As time has gone on we've listened to so many stories about each other's lives that we've begun to feel we've shared a lot, but on that afternoon on the hill at Manly we were still both hovering over the relationship.

In mid-afternoon there was a longish silence. We both gazed out across Manly to the ocean. I thought I'd take the plunge. Why not begin the relationship on a firm, frank footing before awkward expectations were built up?

'You realise, Yvonne, that Peter and I live together, don't you?' There was a slight pause and then she said almost exactly what I would've said in the same circumstances: 'What do you mean by "live together"?' It had been many years since I'd had to choose my words so carefully. 'Well,' I said, 'I mean we're a couple.'

There was another longish pause. 'I see,' she said, and I knew she was suddenly seeing the jigsaw from a completely different angle and that it was causing her, if not pain, then some serious disquiet.

'But surely you suspected?' I said. I even felt a little irritated, I remember. 'I mean, this house ... the way we talk to each other ... '

'No, it never occurred to me. Lots of young men share houses. It never occurred to me.' She didn't sound bewildered, just thoughtful.

'But surely ... I mean, on television, *Number 96*, the soapies, the films ... you can hardly avoid the subject nowadays. It must at least have popped into your mind as a possibility.'

'No, it didn't,' she said firmly, 'that's on television. It's never happened before *in our family*.' Now, it's a large family, Yvonne is one of seven brothers and sisters, they all have several children, some of the children have children, there are dozens and dozens of in-laws … I didn't want to have an argument, but I didn't want to be left appearing the family freak, either.

'Well, I think you'd find,' I said, treading as delicately as I could, 'that at some point somewhere along the line someone had at least given it a go.'

'It's funny you should say that,' she said, with an edge to her voice, 'because I always did wonder about …' (naming here a relative I couldn't place). And we both laughed. So far so good.

It's amazing, isn't it, how easily, how generously a mother can shift her focus in seconds from decades of social conditioning, religious teaching, media clichés and family dogma to focus on one question: is my child happy? It had happened to me once before. Some time after my marriage had broken up and I'd begun to explore the possibilities of emotional and sexual satisfaction with men, I thought I'd better tell my mother-in-law. I wanted to tell her. She was at that time still the only mother figure in my life and I wanted her understanding. She was slicing carrots for dinner one evening in the kitchen of the vicarage in South Yarra. As she sliced, I told her I thought I preferred men sexually. She too came up with some version of 'I see' and kept slicing. Nothing changed. I didn't sense as much as a hiccup in the flow of her affection or attachment. As a vicar's wife she couldn't have been expected to give me her blessing or approval, nor was I looking for either. I wanted a sign that she didn't think any less of me. And she gave it to me. There was no anguished discussion, no raking over the marriage with her daughter, no sermon, just an unbroken flow of the feelings that had been there before I'd spoken. It's miraculous, really.

Whether Jean would have felt so at peace with my preference is hard to say. I fear she may have felt she'd failed in the mothering rôle entrusted to her. Acutely conscious of what was said in certain library books about sons who were strongly attached to older mothers, she constantly seemed to be monitoring my progress through adolescence for signs of deviance from some norm. Part of her found joy in what she called my 'sensitivity' (although she warned me I'd 'suffer for it') and was appalled by some drawings of mine she stumbled across in the margins of an old *Daily Telegraph* of naked, heavy-breasted women. But another part of her, I'm sure, prayed it would all turn out all right—that the adoption would be seen as a success.

For all Yvonne's generosity of spirit, I was aware as I sat with her on the balcony that sweltering afternoon that she still had fears and anxieties that required *my* understanding. One anxiety might be that by letting me be adopted she had left me in moral danger or had caused me some emotional damage resulting in sexual damage—I didn't know her well enough to be sure. So slowly, over an hour or so, I started to explain two things: firstly, that I didn't feel 'damaged' in any way—on the contrary, I felt remarkably whole—and, secondly, that she should not feel remotely responsible for who

I'd turned out to be. I'm not sure she's ever quite believed me on either count. Nor am I sure any more it's as simple as I made it sound. But different occasions have their own truths. And as she left the house towards the end of the afternoon to walk down the hill to the ferry, she stepped up to Peter and gave him a kiss. To you it may have looked like any other kiss. To me it was momentous.

❖ ❖ ❖

One of the things I said to Yvonne that day which I now have doubts about is that I had *chosen* to live as a homosexual. It's not exactly the wrong word, I now think, but it's a word which inadequately describes what happens. Only the most single-minded rebel against the phallocracy, surely, would *choose* (in the ordinary meaning of 'I think I'll take that one') to be a homosexual. At the end of the twentieth century, however, it's become important that people see themselves as authentic constructions, see self, not as a God-given essence, but as the point of intersection of a variety of discourses (conversations going on in society and in your head about who you properly are or should or could be). Freedom, if it means anything, seems to be about choosing intelligently between discourses, questioning commands, interrogating clichéd propositions and making sure what intersects is what you want to intersect. You learn to distinguish between liberating and oppressive discourses. Many of these discourses are rooted in language, naturally enough—'good children love their parents', for example—and so the greater your linguistic sophistication, the greater your ability to interrogate dubious propositions and to ask what 'good' might mean in this case, for instance, or 'love', not to mention 'parents'.

Other, less malleable ideas about what the self might be are scarcely entertained just at the moment by those in the know in my sorts of circles. Some highly educated people, particularly in the humanities, who have no problem with innate gender differences in their own dogs or parrots and seem happy about cows behaving like cows and bulls like bulls (thanks to genetic engineering) jack up when the conversation turns to human animals, animals that use language and plan and dream. It's not as a rule that they deny that biology plays a part in the functioning of all human organs, including the brain, it's just that if you admit that biology plays a major (sometimes any) role in determining who we are as individuals the social engineers amongst us start to lose their sense of power. The idea that the world is all 'text' and you have a leading rôle in writing it is obviously appealing. And while the proposition that you are a linguistic genius for biological reasons is not particularly threatening to anyone, and even the ideological hard-liner with a linguistically gifted child might let it pass unchallenged, the proposition that for much the same reasons you are a homosexual is widely resisted. Some cultural materialists, cocooned in a silky web of social control fantasies, even deny that there was such a thing as homosexuality before the term was coined in the late nineteenth century. And, of course, they're right, there wasn't. But there was something we'd *now* call homosexuality long before the term was coined—men preferring sex with other men, women desiring mainly or only women—just as there were koalas before anyone called them koalas.

So why do so many intellectuals of my generation resist the notion that homosexuality, say, as opposed to nose-length or glaucoma may be genetically determined? After all, can there be anything as likely to be genetically determined as sexuality? The usual answer that's given is that the 'world as text' view, in which even AIDS becomes a metaphor for something else, gives us freedom to change our world. Biology is so fixed, it takes away the possibility of choice. I don't really buy that argument. For a start, biology is dangerously unfixed and the possibility of choice increases almost daily. No, I think the cultural materialist's rejection of biology comes down to a desire to salvage something from Marxism, from that nineteenth century dream of a socially engineered, just society. It also comes, I think, from the conviction amongst the language-based professionals—historians and English Literature lecturers in particular—that if they play their cards right they can dictate the text. They're simply not equipped to dictate biology. I think it's about power and power's considerable rewards.

I was a staunch believer in the world-as-text approach from about the mid-sixties, when I first encountered Bakhtin and the structuralists, until quite recently. For almost twenty years. Even in my metaphysical musings, 'in the beginning was the Word' invited multiple readings. God created by 'saying', by naming, and in the *maya* world of illusion, Adam (human consciousness) created by renaming. After meeting Yvonne, though, and watching the way she sits and walks, listening to her talk and tell jokes, looking at photographs of my half-brother (he even stands like me) and thinking back over my life in order to be able to explain it to her, I find it an unconvincing view of human nature and who we are—beautiful and ripe for exploitation by people like me, but at best only part of the picture. Social forces may largely determine the form a preference for one's own sex takes, but I now doubt that it always produces it in the first place.

Like almost every gay male I've read or heard talk on the subject, I was aware from earliest childhood of an attraction to males which excited my genitals. It happened at such an early age—I can still remember dreaming clammy dreams at five or six about the man next door, desiring genital contact—that I find it hard to understand except in terms of some innate disposition. Perhaps it's a disposition everyone has but most are socialised out of dwelling on or developing. But in conversation most gay males I've heard speak about it do so in order to emphasise the point that 'that's the way I was from the start'. To quote the historian Garry Wotherspoon, 'my homoerotic interests were a given for me', although I doubt he would approve of the use I'm making of his declaration.

From a very early age—certainly under six—I was aware of being different, although I hardly knew from what. I knew that the cards I'd been dealt (by circumstance, biology, whatever agency) made up an odd hand. You notice at school that you speak differently (and differently from your parents), you notice you speak just a little too *well*. ('Are you English, son?' one teacher asked me in fourth class and it wasn't a friendly question, despite the maps of the British Empire on the classroom wall. It was an invitation to climb down a peg or two.) You notice in yourself a certain fastidiousness that discomforts people, an attention to dress, as it used to be phrased, that isn't quite ... what? You notice other boys don't mind tearing their clothes off in the changing-sheds and knocking each other about (but you do), other boys enjoy winning things—matches, races, card-games, anything (you don't much), other boys think smacking a cricket-ball around an oval is fun (you find it boring and pointless). Above all, you notice other boys like being with other boys. You basically like being with girls.

Although none of us could have quite put our finger on it at the time, Jean and Tom must have noticed I was not growing up to be a real man. They sent me to Scouts on Friday nights, they made me go to tennis lessons on Saturday mornings, they encouraged me to make friends with other little boys and inspect their model trains and cicada collections, they gave me all the building blocks they could to make a real man of me, but I didn't build anything with them. Tom, strangely (the pub owner's son, merchant seaman, radio operator and, in his old age, messenger boy for an advertising company) didn't seem much concerned.

As I got older and drifted off into my various Pure Lands, my failure to connect with normal boyhood became more marked, although I don't remember being bullied or made to suffer for it. Nowadays I read all these memoirs about how other little boys went fishing with their fathers, killed things, pulled little girls' (and little boys') knickers down behind sheds in hot backyards, and later got drunk on Saturday nights with their mates from the football club and cruised around Kings Cross leering at prostitutes. I didn't do any of that. I did get infatuated with dreamy girls from private schools at dancing classes at the local Masonic Hall (I excelled at the cha-cha, possibly for genetic reasons) but on the whole I had far more important, more thrilling things on my mind (I thought) than pulling down girls' knickers or getting drunk. I would wander the streets after school or on a Saturday afternoon talking to myself or the dog in my secret language, literally reinterpreting the universe, making up a medieval history for my Shambhala, trying to work out what it meant to say that God was both All and also spirit, or thinking about Communism, Hungary, Tibet, who Jesus was, rehearsing conversations with real and imaginary friends, making up far-fetched, dangerous stories about my origins—I was swimming in an ocean of words in several languages. I knew this was strange, I knew that even at Sunday School the other boys were different and thought a lot about girls and cars and cricket and having a good time, but I was only vaguely aware that the way I was had sexual implications. I didn't know you had to be one thing or the other (a notion some gay activists, paradoxically, have energetically reaffirmed, with excellent results in terms of their own career prospects).

The first time these implications were spelt out to me—the first time I realised my difference disgusted people—was in college in Canberra. I was eighteen. It was my first year away from home. One night in early winter at about ten o'clock I left my room to take a walk around the grounds and breathe in a bit of frosty air. I always read in the evenings, I never, needless to say, played billiards or went off in a group to the pub. I'd hardly gone two yards down the darkened corridor when I heard my name mentioned behind a closed door opposite. I stopped to listen. Some beery, smoky gathering of the boys. 'What a bloody poof *he* is!' I went cold. 'Yeah, let's teach the little queer a lesson!' 'D'you know what he did the other day? He was behind me in the queue in the servery and he bumped his tray up against mine like this— *bump! bump!* I got the message. Little shit!' I was starting to feel nauseated and leant against the wall by the door. 'Yeah, let's teach him a lesson. Let's take him out into the bush, rip his clothes off and leave him there. Fucking poof.'

I went back to my room in a sick daze. I was trembling with the shock of it. I locked the door and lay down on my bed and simply wept. (Which is what you'd expect a queer to do, after all.) What distressed me wasn't just the sickening thought that these boys I said hullo to as we passed on the footpath or sat next to at table took it I was homosexual and desired them (I wasn't and didn't), it was as much as anything the violent hatred. Why did they hate me so much? I wasn't in any state to reflect on the irony of a group of young men choosing to sit around together discussing another male's sexuality and fantasising about stripping him naked and sexually degrading him.

My solution was a Christian one: stare out the evil until it retreats, kill it with kindness. I'd heard the boy who lived in that room say he always had trouble waking up in the morning, his alarm-clock having no effect, so the next day I said to him that, if he liked, I'd wake him every morning on the way to breakfast. And he agreed. And I did it for the rest of the term. Curious, isn't it? And the only open sexual harassment I experienced that year was from the father of one of the boys in the room that night. He chased me around the table in his professorial office three times in an ungainly effort to press his suit.

What I didn't understand in those days, the early 'sixties, was that in any society ideas about what constitutes masculinity and what constitutes femininity are rigidly fixed and the boundary between them is jealously guarded. It's a binary system and one that confers power. The economic and political structure, and the rewards system in particular, are based on those ideas, making any movement in them dangerous. Sometimes you might go to a country where masculinity and femininity are defined differently—to Turkey, say, or Russia—and at first it seems liberating and exciting. So it *is* possible to be a man, after all, and hold hands with your best friend, so it *is* possible to be a man and love poetry, talk about God and death instead of cars, drink no alcohol, go to art galleries with your friends on Saturday afternoons instead of football matches ... Then it dawns on you that the lines between real men and real women are just as rigidly drawn in Turkey and Russia as they are at home, and are just as jealously guarded (perhaps more so), they're just drawn in a different place.

Here in Australia until quite recently you were either masculine or you were feminine. It was a package deal. A man looked hard-edged—rough-hewn, perhaps, but hard-edged—haircut, forehead, nose, chin, chest ... Lower down certain allowances were made (a soft belly was a sign of other manly activities, after all), but the public parts of the anatomy should be sharp. A man was emotionally and linguistically restrained, not given to talking about his feelings, except in orgiastic outbursts, which made alcohol every true man's accessory, although he could talk about his health at a fairly crude physical level—'I feel crook', 'I feel great' and so on. A man was attuned to physical sensations rather than to sensitivities (the smell and sounds of the garden or bush, the taste of good food, sexual sensations—but not to describing them *too well*); he was physically hardworking (he built, he cleared, he rode, he laboured—he was not a dainty clerk or a librarian); he dominated nature by thrusting into it, killing things, turning forest into farmland, building cities, laying railway tracks, flying planes, dousing fires, steering ships across oceans—he didn't decorate, write commentaries, embroider or colour in; he didn't keep

clean and tidy except on active combat duty, preferring to clean
up massively once a month; and he was a realist, engaging with
the world face to face, calling a spade a spade, laying it on the
line—he had no patience with metaphysics, fictions, poetic
transformations, ironic transgressions—with art, in other
words. And in each of these categories I failed the test. I
felt, I talked, I mooned, I wrote, I embroidered, I tidied
away, I lived in a meta-universe. The real thing was grist to my
transforming mill.

I expect the boys in college that night had seen all this, as
I had not, and put two and two together and concluded I was,
in Australian terms, a girl. And so doubly disgusting: to be
reviled both as a girl and as a boy who chose to be a girl. I was
therefore, on both counts, fit to be violated.

Few of us, I think, are unsinning in this regard, if a
little less crudely than the boys in that room that night. How
easy it is to catch yourself thinking there's something
slightly effeminate ('poofy') about long-haired men, say,
who fight against the domination of nature by other men,
who carry on about rain forests and use natural healing
methods. How easy it is to jump to conclusions about the
sexuality of a man who prefers going to the ballet or reading
a novel to fixing the car or even tinkering in the shed.
There's always a small suspicion in the back of the mind
about a man who chooses his words too carefully, who
plays with ironies or cadences, who too readily finds the
precise word to express his feelings about a friend or a
painting. It used to be called 'ambiguity', such a man was

'ambiguous'—and indeed he was, because the signals he sent out could be read in two ways.

On that May night in college in 1962, however, I was not equipped to consider these questions quite as rationally. I didn't see myself as a queer, a poof, a homosexual, a non-man. What I said to myself was that basically I liked spending my time with girls, talking with them, going out with them, dancing with them, touching them, kissing them, not realising that this in itself was a mark against me. Girls were for wooing, penetrating and marrying, not for merging with; perhaps when you were old and married it didn't matter so much any more, but not when you were young, sharp as a blade, honed to action and to carving out a space in the world.

At the same time I was forced that night to confront and interpret the fact that although I was emotionally bound up with many women, I was drawn to maleness as well and found it sexually exciting at times. I was drawn to it in a fugitive, dreamlike way, almost as if I caught myself listening in sometimes to someone else's whispers.

Man as knife, that was the nub of it. I even remember when still a boy finding the Russian word for the dagger wild Circassian tribesmen used erotic. *Kinzhal*. Keen Zhal. *Zhalo*: a sting, a prick, the point of a needle. There was a vengeful *kinzhal* in every Romantic tale of lust and derring-do I read—Pushkin, Lermontov, Tolstoy. They were slipped in, plunged in, twisted in, the victim writhed and groaned and then there was bloody silence. I was not knife-like. Only

my tongue was sharp-edged and that, although I didn't
know it, was a woman's attribute.

But I saw knives on buses, on the screen, in the schoolyard,
behind shop counters, collecting fares. I saw them and felt
drawn to their hard edges, but only hazily. I had very little idea
of what taking one of these knives into myself might mean.
Looking at one across an aisle or a shop-counter (and I was not
always as furtive about that as I should have been), I wished
more that I could bring that cutting edge out in myself.
Perhaps then I, too, could learn to hack, clear, cut, plunge and
jab.

Not that I was a roly-poly beach-ball of a child with a
puddingy face and a Cupid's penis. Not at all. I had some
knife-like possibilities, but I was small. More your butter-knife
with a fine bone handle than your Oriental dagger. Small
and slightly woppish. 'Stand up, Jones, and show the class
what "sallow" means,' said Mr L. when I was in fifth class. I
stood up and thought of myself as displeasingly sallow for the
next twenty years. No one ever asked me to demonstrate
what 'olive-skinned' meant.

Of course, a smooth olive skin, strong cheek-bones and
thinnish body (good calves) appealed to some. I couldn't
help noticing. But until I started reading André Gide I was
very unclear about what this appeal might lead to. My
mother had warned me specifically about those men on
park benches wearing socks with sandals. She'd said nothing,
however, about Latin masters who asked me home after
school for private lessons with knee-squeezing thrown in, or

about smartly dressed men with account addresses in Double Bay and Vaucluse—customers in the bookshop in Castlereagh Street—who wondered what time I finished work and if I'd like to 'do something' when the shop closed. She'd said not a word about boys in football jerseys at bustops blowing gum-bubbles who asked me where I lived and if I had a girlfriend and what time my mother got home. Most particularly, she hadn't warned me to be on the lookout for the blatant approach of the three young men I helped with maps one sultry afternoon in the bookstore. It must have been about 1960. They were blades, in body-hugging T-shirts, strong legs in rough material, dirty boots. They were off across the Nullarbor to Perth. A bit of horseplay over the maps. Gary was the clown, the lair. 'Hey, Rod,' he said, jabbing a thumb half over his shoulder at me, 'ya wannim?' Rod lowered the map of the Nullarbor and looked me over from head to foot. He scratched at his crotch, raised the map and said: 'Nah, too small.' I was mildly disappointed, I think, as much as affronted or disgusted. Not that I'd have gone off with Rod even if he'd given me the nod—there was no place for that in any of my scripts. If anything, I was intrigued that such people could exist: young men in T-shirts, manly young men who drove cars across the Nullarbor, not Classics masters or grubby, confused boys in the backs of buses, but ordinary young men who apparently had sex with other ordinary young men, perhaps even their ordinary mates, yet weren't riven or anguished or furtive or freakish. They'd made a mistake, needless to say, in thinking I might be available to join in such activities—I wasn't and never would be available—but it was intriguing nonetheless.

In none of my Pure Lands was there any place for a homosexual. In my God-is-All world neither God nor His infinite manifestation was sexual at all (there being neither male nor female in the Christian heaven—that is, in the consciousness of absolute reality) and if in the human dream about God and His manifestation there were finite bodies with sexual urges, this was best dealt with through a loving, companionate uniting of the male and female. I didn't see in those days how those butter-soft words surreptitiously underpinned a whole political and economic structure (socialist, capitalist, it didn't matter, it was everywhere the same). Nor did homosexuals appear in the streets of my other Pure Land, my Shambhala—not in the bohemian quarter of the city of K., in the monasteries, on the farms, in the shops or hotels or theatres—it was almost as if I instinctively knew that if men are to rule (as they naturally did there), they must establish what makes a man a man and jealously define and guard the difference. Queen Victorias in mauve suits, like Mr J. in Hardback Fiction, were no threat to the line, nor were simpering, knee-squeezing Latin masters waxing lyrical about Virgil, nor were greasy adolescents, poking about inside their flies, or softly spoken bookreaders, for that matter, with tasteful flats in Double Bay and a penchant for French art films. They were all clowns, Black and White Minstrels, parodying the Other, highlighting the division between masculine and feminine;

indeed, in some ways probably entrenching it.

In Russia, my other Land, homosexuals simply didn't exist. They were painted over, married off, enveloped in silence. Russia was the land of realist fictions, after all, which thrives on heterosexual arrangements—they produce such marvellously continuous narratives. In Russian fiction by and large men acted and women were acted upon: thesis, antithesis, synthesis/thesis, antithesis, synthesis, all pleasingly dialectical. Well, there were some *strong* women in Russian fiction: in Turgenev's *Rudin*, for example, and in his *Fathers and Sons*, in *War and Peace, Crime and Punishment,* even Chekhov's plays. On the whole, however, the women's strength was severely virginal, needing fertilisation by a male in order to produce anything of value, even if the male in question proved hopeless at doing anything at all. Or else their strength was nothing more than a destructive excess of sexual energy. Pushkin's Tatyana in *Eugene Onegin* showed a bit of initiative, it's true—she wrote to Onegin and scandalously declared her love, and later as an unhappily married woman she refused an affair with him, which showed some kind of strength of character—but she was scarcely a feminist heroine. At the symbolic level, particularly, Russia in my day was the land of gigantic statues of bronze heroes thrusting forwards, the land of generals and marshals and gangs of muscled workmen damming rivers and pushing through the trackless *taiga*.

All the same, in real life and even in art from time to time, Russian men could be disconcertingly unknife-like.

Masculinity in Russian seemed to allow for things it didn't allow for in Australia. It seemed to allow for sentimentality, for example, for a love of language and poetry and painting, for strong emotional attachments to other men, for a certain physical flabbiness, for laziness and lying about. Things that made men ambiguous in our society didn't seem to make them ambiguous in Russia. A man might be 'womanish' in some regard—he might drift about in a reverie, for example, talking too much and too self-consciously well, he might dress with too much care for the effect, or show more interest in courtship and romance than in actually having sex—without showing any interest at all in sexual relations with other men. I heard jokes about the men who loitered in the park in front of the Bolshoi Theatre and jokes about Tchaikovsky, a smutty story or two about Pushkin (a skirt-chaser if ever there was one) and a rumour about Gogol, but by and large in Russia, at least in my time, even amongst my actor friends, men were men and women were women and there was no confusion in their minds about the difference. Sex lined up pretty well with gender. Not a single officially published novel, poem, short story or play, not a film on any screen, not an article in any newspaper, no history text, no limerick, no biography, no radio interview ever mentioned homosexuality.

In conversation, on the rare occasions it came up, it was exoticised, as it was in Australia until quite recently. It was said to flourish in the Caucasus, for example, and in Central Asia, both 'illicit zones' in the Russian imagination. 'In

Yerevan,' my swarthy Armenian neighbour Vil once said to me after one cognac too many, 'if my friend and I see a cute couple necking in the park, I'll say to him: "Tell you what: I'll take the girl and you can take the boy."' Raucous laughter. I didn't react. I think the Foreign Department had asked him to feel me out. ('Vil', by the way, stood for 'Vladimir Ilyich Lenin'—they chose our neighbours for us very carefully at Moscow University. I wonder if he's changed his name.) Homosexuality was also a foreign condition, meaning Western, bred in the fetid atmosphere of late capitalism, and it was of some interest to the KGB who thought they could exploit it to their own purposes. One of my fellow students that first year, on exchange from London University, was photographed by the KGB in bed with another male. They thought they could blackmail him by threatening to send copies to his parents in England. He simply asked for additional copies for himself and his friends. The KGB never understood the 'sixties. Nor, as I've said, did I.

The only friend I made at Moscow University with any real awareness of deviant sexuality was an Estonian student I'll call Arvo. We met when I was on telephone duty on our floor of the student hostel. I was sitting at the telephone desk, taking calls and buzzing students to come to the phone, and between calls Arvo engaged me in the kind of conversation only Balts seemed to know how to make. Despite over two decades of Soviet Communism and energetic Russian colonisation, Estonians in particular always seemed to me utterly unaffected, completely 'Western' in their thinking—

Hanseatic, Scandinavian, Germanic, anything but Soviet. It was like talking to a well-read, highly educated young man from Berlin or Stockholm. He could sense who I was, he could read my signals in a way most Russians could not. He was modern—Russians seemed so stuck somewhere in the 1890s, pre-Freud, pre-Jung, pre-twentieth century. Not gay, but queer. Married, naturally, with a child. A cultural historian, knowledgeable about Islam. Apart from a *frisson* or two, no sexual relationship developed from that first conversation by the telephone desk, but a lifelong friendship did, with many visits to Tallinn and an affection, if not a deeply informed one, for Estonian fiction, poetry and painting. I've always liked little countries, you see—perhaps I hear echoes in them of my own Shambhala. Iceland, Estonia, Lithuania, Andorra, Ecuador—you can take them in whole and know them intimately, as loved narratives.

I actually had a strong attachment that first year in Russia to one of my classmates, a girl called Natasha. I don't think Arvo quite approved of it. The KGB made no obvious objections, which is probably one of the reasons Arvo didn't quite approve of it. I'm not sure, looking back, how passionate it was on my part, but as the year progressed I sought out her company more and more, or she mine, even spending the occasional night at her flat or one of her friends'. We courted in the way couples did in Russian textbooks of the period, in the exercises on declensions and verb endings: 'Natasha, would you like to go to the cinema?' 'Yes, I would. There's a very good film on at the

Kosmos. Would you like to see it?' Or: 'Let's invite some friends to dinner at my place. I have some meat, some cucumber and some potatoes.' 'Good. I'll buy some ice-cream. Then we can play some music and dance.' In accordance with this rather stilted script we went to the opera and the ballet, to fine restaurants and snack-bars, to apartment blocks all over Moscow visiting friends, and because Natasha was reasonably 'well-connected', she brooked no argument from the kind of people whose full-time job it was in those days to keep the general public at bay—to stop theatre-lovers seeing plays, book-lovers buying books, travellers buying tickets and diners forcing their way into half-full restaurants and eating the food the staff was selling at black market prices out the back door, and so on. Natasha could get into a restaurant that was literally barracaded against the public like a medieval fortress. Within half an hour we would be ensconced inside eating our cabbage soup. For people of Natasha's class a deficit economy had definite social advantages. It was a source of power and privilege, and I'm not surprised that many of them want it back.

For the serious courting couple sleeping together at the hostel could be a risky business, not to mention the discomfort of single beds. You have to understand that half the country wanted to live in Moscow, the seat of power in a highly cen-tralised state, where the standard of living was comparatively high, but to live in Moscow you needed a residence permit and that was almost impossible to obtain, unless you had a job in Moscow or were born there or had married a Muscovite.

That's why you saw forty-year-old actresses playing the Three Sisters in repertory at the Moscow Arts Theatre—they had their job and their flat in Moscow and they weren't going to move to Omsk or Tomsk or Irkutsk for anything in the world. Integrity is not a Russian concept; they make do with honesty. So massive sweeps were occasionally arranged without warning of the entire eighteen storeys of the student hostel to clean out illicit residents. Not only was the building sealed off from top to bottom by squads of young Party activists, the various zones or sections were also individually sealed off, as was each floor. The lifts were stopped and the staircases were locked. Then the room-by-room search began. By the end of the night on one occasion in 1967 some 1,600 illegal residents had been found and sent packing—grandmothers up from the country, packs of children, nephews, cousins, wives from Vladivostok, old school friends moonlighting on some building site. By the early hours of the morning the population of a large village found itself standing outside in the frost looking back at the illuminated Stalinist wedding-cake soaring up into the sky, a forbidden zone. So there were restrictions on courting and a lot of it took place amongst the marble columns of the underground stations.

As far as Natasha was concerned, though, at the back of my mind was the fear that she wanted to marry me and get out. Marriage only really started to seem attractive to me once I got back to Australia in late 1967, back to the bungalows, backyards, family cars and furnishing departments in well-stocked department stores. Falling in love, marrying, building a house, children, family Christmases—it was a plot, a folk-tale I could imagine falling in with once back in Canberra. And I did, although I didn't quite get to the end of the story.

One night in 1968 I fell in love instantly and for about twelve years. I was showing slides of the Soviet Union to a group of students in a friend's flat. It was exotic in those days to have travelled to Samarkand and Tbilisi, Kiev and Tallinn and to have lived in Moscow for a year without being a fellow-traveller. At about eight o'clock the wire back-door opened and Elizabeth walked in. Before the door had even clicked shut again, I was in love. Totally and until about 1980. I still remember the door snapping shut *after* the bolt of obsessive love had struck. By midnight, at home again, drinking tea heavily, I'd determined to marry this Elizabeth, this beautiful, fragile, glassy-edged churchman's daughter. And I did, eighteen months later, in the little Anglican church on the hill overlooking the sea at Gerringong, where Tom was still living, now a widower. Tom thought Elizabeth was a princess. Her father married us. I suppose it was a mistake in some sense, at least from Elizabeth's point of view. But I'm not sure what 'mistake' really means in this context. I don't regret it for a single second.

What can I put my instantaneous obsession down to, except some sort of Rorschach effect? I can't think of any other explanation. Slowly, over years, some sort of inky blob runs and dries, runs and dries in your mind, bulging here because of some Pepsi ad, trickling down there because of someone you saw on a bus, zigzagging here wildly because of an overpoweringly erotic experience when you were twelve, turning pink there because of all those nineteenth-century Russian novels you'd read and so on. Gradually, over twenty years, if you're basically introverted, darting in and out of the world only to borrow books and meet others in highly constructed situations, this blob *becomes* your object of desire. So, if a door opens and this blob appears, walks in and smiles at you, you're thunderstruck, instantly attached, desperate to merge with, fit around this blob and stay there for all eternity. It's pathetic, really. It's also like being struck with lightning and surviving, unable to comprehend your astounding good fortune, your billion-to-one against-the-odds survival.

And you're always busy, too, because the actual woman or man never *really* fits the blob in every detail. So the obsessive can spend years on a daily basis chipping away at the disparities, remoulding here, thinking wishfully there, squashing this bit in and pretending that bit isn't there at all. You, the obsessed, don't have to change. It's not so much that you are perfect (so sniping on that score misses the mark), it's more that you're not there at all. You're a ravenous eye on the alert for quiverings of change in your beloved, for any sign that blob and beloved are not one. As an eye you're seen by others as single-minded and self-centred, but to itself the eye is just an eye, a focus of experience. It doesn't occur to you, as an eye, that you have to *do* anything. It's madness.

And so, years after we were married, I'd still find myself at home some afternoons, waiting for Elizabeth to drive round the curve in the road and up our drive and be home, almost unable to breathe until she got there. I'd stand and stare out the window up the empty Canberra street, feeling somehow unplugged until she got home and turned the switch and I could observe again. To this day I feel faintly sick at heart when I hear a car's tyres crunching on a gravel drive.

We did *do* things, naturally. We built a house in a new suburb of Canberra with a wonderful sharp-edged view across to the Brindabellas, a view I wrote my first published poem about, after filtering it through Mandelstam. We holidayed on a house-boat in Kashmir and we lived in Moscow together for six months, in one tiny room at Moscow University with only a single bed for both of us. The question of a double bed seemed to embarrass the authorities into blank silence. We lived for a while in Vapaaniemi on the forested, snowy edges of Helsinki while I read in the library; we lived in Paris for six months, again while I read in the library; we caught trains around Europe—Bulgaria, Rumania, Berlin, Sweden, Turkey, Poland, we were very mobile. Some would say it was an interesting, even exciting life. I didn't drink or run after other women, we shared the household chores, we talked a lot and read and had nice educated friends and pottered in the garden and never had flaming rows. But in the end I didn't fit Elizabeth's Rorschach blob, not by a long shot, and never had. So she'd never been *in love* with me. It's heart-wrenching to have to acknowledge that—it cuts you to the quick.

Obsession makes marriage impossible, I admit. It can add dramatic punch and narrative thrust to an affair, but it bogs a marriage down in repetition, circling, movement inwards towards a point where sacred stories are retold over and over again in a private language whose syntax allows no deviation. You panic at any sign that your object of desire is not conforming to the Ur-blob—scorns aspects of your spiritual system, for example, likes drinking wine, dislikes some of your close friends (perfectly decent, right-thinking people), has fears and anxieties about silly things like sickness and ageing and the pointlessness of everything, things you've explained the answers to a thousand times. And so you're seen as intolerant, while all the time you see yourself as just seeing.

And because your blob-beloved fills your whole field of vision twenty-four hours a day—gives meaning to making toast (she'll smell it and eat it), missing a bus (half an hour lost from your time with her), filling the car with petrol (for her to drive around in, lighting up the city as she passes—no, truly)—because, like sun-worship, nothing you do is ever unrelated to this central fact of your existence, a terrifying burden settles on your love.

As if the burden of my obsessive love were not nightmare enough, there was another burden Elizabeth, fragile but with hard edges, had to bear after Jean and Tom had died. To the introvert, incessantly aware of no-father, no-mother, no-brother, no-sister (I don't know how else to put it—you're aware of a very specific kind of absence), a wife is called upon to be, as well as lover and companion, an understanding, monitoring mother (approached with gooey baby words when very insecure), sister (unquestioningly bound to you, not to be penetrated, partner in pranks) and loyal friend—a distasteful combination, when you think about it.

This particular burden was made heavier by Jean's incarceration and death in 1969, while we were living in Sydney, courting—that is, seeing each other almost every day and experimenting with our sexual tastes. I suppose that's what courting means, or perhaps it was more a matter of my wooing her. Jean's was a dreadful, gruelling death—I'd rather be shot or starve to death than die like that.

She'd been getting dottier and gaunter for years. When I came back from a month's hiking holiday in New Zealand in 1964, she seemed convinced I'd been gone two years. 'Why did you stay away so long?' she asked reproachfully, tears in her voice. 'Why did you never write, never get in touch with us? And we love you so very much!' In fact I'd written almost every day—Tom wrapped all my letters and cards up in a little bundle which I've kept to this day. Tom and I largely pretended nothing was happening. Apart from anything else, I've always been a coward where madness is concerned. I can smell it in a room, I can smell it getting on a bus to choose a seat across the aisle. It always infuriated me to hear clever young things with a couple of French philosophers under their belt seriously suggesting it was we who were mad and the sane who were locked up in asylums, it being all an oppressive social construct. Asylums have always been used to lock up the subversive and peculiar, of course, definitions of madness have always been adapted to suit the reigning ideology and how we use the word 'mad' shifts according to the time and place. But it's not *just* a social construct. Living with Jean was living with madness and it became unbearable.

Our intolerance had other roots, though, it wasn't just cowardice. It was also ignorance and fear. Jean had, after all, had that nervous breakdown before I was born, spending two years virtually locked inside the house, standing at the sink washing her hands until they were raw and swollen. So she was flawed. Then when they moved to Gerringong, a small village on the coast south of Wollongong, while I was in Russia, Jean started writing me heart-wrenching letters, the lines veering off at mad angles towards the corners of the pages, calmly panic-stricken letters, misspelt, sometimes with no signature. She felt, I think, that she'd washed up, after a life of minor humiliations, like a piece of rubbish on a deserted beach. You couldn't talk to Tom about it. He was nearly eighty, blissfully at peace with himself and the world. His days were filled with winning chook raffles at the bowling club and ambling up the green hill to the shop with the dog, the ocean shining and thudding behind his back. He loved to mag, as Carmel Bird would say, over the fence to the neighbours or sit on the front verandah in his Hawaiian shirt with *Marlborough's French Phrase Book* or the morning newspaper in his lap, tossing jocular remarks at passers-by. 'He became a popular resident through his most jovial personality,' as the obituary in the local newspaper worded it, 'and his kindness and friendliness as a neighbour.'

Jean started saying 'pass the boot' instead of 'pass the butter', trying to cook in the refrigerator, forgetting how to do up buttons, mistaking me for Tom and other things that made you weep. I still dream, to this very day, of Jean coming to the table in the morning, the sea gleaming like a metal sheet through the venetians, and saying 'pass the butter, please' and finding all her words fall into place and all of us laughing until we cry from joy.

Eventually, Jean had to be 'looked after'. Well, I suppose she really did. Tom was emotionally out of his depth and, eighty now (but quite rotund and lively), he could not be expected to bathe and dress and feed his ever madder wife and sit with her all day staring out through the venetians. He never read, apart from French grammars and phrase-books, occasionally an old dictionary flattened silverfish used to drop out of, and the newspaper. So Jean was committed to a psychiatric hospital in Sydney. Since I was living there, teaching Russian, a half-hour's drive away on the other side of the harbour, it was left to me to visit her. Elizabeth very often came with me. I think Tom only saw her once during the nine months or so she took to die.

I used to go five or six times a week. When I lost my driving-licence for sliding down a slippery wet hill into the back of another car, I started going on the bus, an hour each way, sitting upstairs at the front teaching myself Polish to pass the time. I suppose I went because I wanted to protect her as best I could from any sense of being abandoned or left unloved. I think that scarifying final scene in *The Cherry Orchard* was lurking in my mind, too. If you've ever seen the play, you'll remember it—it's the archetypally horrifying ending: Firs the decrepit family retainer is left locked up and forgotten in the house when Ranevskaya and her self-indulgent entourage pack up and leave forever. When I got to Gladesville, Jean would be propped up like a scarecrow in a washed-out nightie in a large, bare room with other lunatics, perhaps eating if I was a little late. The sick and mad in our society, as you'll have noticed, are always fed early, like children, and then dropped into the yawning night to confront their fears alone, constantly a few hours out of kilter with the normal world. Sometimes she'd know who I was and we'd have a kind of lurching conversation about this and that, sometimes she'd take me for Tom or her brother or not know me at all and get petulant. Sometimes she seemed to be all too aware of this ultimate humiliation in her life, this final debasement of what was fine in her. She'd pick at her grubby hospital nightie and say to me: 'I look like a clown, don't I?' It made my throat burn with tears and I couldn't speak. One afternoon when I got to Gladesville she wasn't there at all. Without a word to anyone (except, perhaps, 'Jean, we're taking you on a little trip, dear—won't that be nice?') she'd been removed to the asylum at Callan Park for some experiments. Almost numb with anxiety I caught a bus to Callan Park (taxis in those days being only for taking luggage to the station). Jean was lying in appalling pain— from what? she wasn't sick—fretting like an animal for ... I don't know what for. Love, succour, comfort, care—no word is intense enough. And all I could do was stroke her and weep, I couldn't reach into her with what she ached for. Then one day she was gone from there, too. Back to Gladesville. They'd finished.

One Sunday afternoon I was sitting with her in her little, white room with its barred window, listening to the clanging and shrieking and the mad piano banging deeper inside the building, not saying much—what was there to say? She was lying chalk-white on her bed by the window. Her breathing seemed to go awry and then she missed a breath and then there was no more breathing. Inside you every fibre of your being starts to scream against the stillness on the bed. But Jean was a story no one ever listened to. And once she'd gone I doubt a single human being ever remembered, or only fleetingly, its being told.

Tom died a couple of years later, but with a certain flair. Elizabeth and I were in Turkey on the day. He was mowing the back grass—he always loved getting the Victa into the long kikuyu, cutting long, shining swathes in the moist lawn—and stopped to go up into the house to write us a letter. I expect it was one of those lovingly long, unplaintive letters of his about all manner of daily things: the dog, the cat, the goat from up the road, the heat or his conversations with the Congregational minister about death and other theological matters. He wrote about half a page and in mid-sentence died. I still have the letter upstairs there somewhere, but I can't read it, so I can't tell you exactly what he said.

By the time I got back from Turkey, Dad had been buried by his friend the Congregational minister, the house was shut up and only the dog, dazed and wobbly, was there in the empty house to greet me. Neighbours had been feeding it. Sterling Christian folk they were, too, the pillars of some local church or other, and the first thing they did as soon as they saw the blinds were up was to send their mentally retarded son across with a bill for the dog food. The real message was that now Tom had gone I didn't belong there.

People are so scathing about Canberra, which is where I did belong and lived out my married life in the early 'seventies. They're scathing about the people they imagine live there, the deathly quiet of the lush suburban streets, the bourgeois comfortableness of the city, its circular streets, the arid new suburbs, its unreality, its lack of a city centre—there's no end to what they're scathing about. I must say I loved living there. Like Berlin (which it's utterly unlike) Canberra appealed to me partly because right there in front of me was a Pure Land in operation—planned, beautiful (lakes, gardens, mountains), ruled by benevolent dictators, not the mob, cleansed of the grosser aspects of capitalism—it was almost classless in a Soviet sort of way (that is, rigidly stratified, but not according to who owned what). The people with status in the community seemed to be members of the intelligentsia—professors and poets and chief librarians, senior civil servants and eminent biologists. God alone knows who built the roads or dug the lake—they just appeared where someone very highly placed had decided they should. Canberra lulled you into thinking all was right with the world. It was the perfect place to be married in.

Homosexuality never really raised its head in Canberra. There was some scandal about a professor taking a young man back to his room in a government hostel, I seem to remember, something about nakedness and violence, but in general it was something that happened in artistic circles elsewhere, amongst the sort of people who read *Nation Review*. It was certainly no threat to my marriage. I'd tried it once in Paris—a young Frenchman offered to help me read my street-map on the Boulevard Clichy, we had a coffee, he came back to my hotel—but I'd hated it, it nauseated me even to think about it. I didn't think it was 'wrong', whatever that meant, or any more 'wrong' than any other kind of self-indulgence, I just didn't enjoy it. And, although I had no theoretical reasoning at my disposal to back my intuition up, I did intuit that to enjoy it was a threat to the social order, to the present comfortable arrangement of happy families with lines of power passing through males to other males right up to the top. It didn't matter much if you wanted to write books or dance in the corps de ballet, but it did matter if you wanted to find a niche in the power structure.

Not enjoying sex with men did not mean that I was not attracted during those married years to certain men. Desire, I suppose, has something to do with the anguish of incompletion, and my incompletion sneered at me from every billboard, every cinema-screen, every novel, every magazine. I could hardly fail to be anguished and therefore to desire.

Real men penetrated, that was the thing. They penetrated with bulldozers, jackhammers, bullets, even pens and telephones, they penetrated goal-posts and cricket-stumps, space in sputniks, the Congo, New Guinea, the Blue Mountains, the line of breakers, they smashed records, barriers, rocks, the established order, the quiet of a suburban afternoon with piercing rock music—and incidentally in passing, they penetrated women. The ideal male body was finely attuned to this task of slicing and penetrating and it appeared more and more everywhere—unsung, in a sense, but depicted and described on television and in books. It was lithe, well-defined, sprang instantly from relaxation into tensile readiness and bore one or two signs of penetrating activity in the past (a scar, perhaps, a broken bone a little crookedly healed, even a very slight limp was acceptably manly).

When I saw real men I felt the anguish and so the desire. A little ambiguity, a little confusion over the signs, could make the anguish grow even more lushly. Jean-Paul Belmondo, for example, whose smooth skin made his manliness all the more piquant. Or a young Moroccan (not a sailor in a bar, where meanings are quite clear) in a flowing, pale-blue jelaba, say, or speaking knowledgeably about the Roman ruins at Volubilis, or even affectionately about his wife. Or a Bulgarian wrestler (I once spent a night on a train in Bulgaria locked in a compartment with five Bulgarian wrestlers, three stripped to the waist)—not in a head-lock, but more ambiguously engaged in self-display or horse-play with his rippling mates. In these sorts of situations, while I was married, I had no desire to penetrate or to be penetrated, I wanted to absorb in some way, merge with, fade into the penetrating masculinity. I would become a mirror, a kind of zero, reflecting back whatever would keep the display of masculinity flowing to feed my desire. But once the object of desire had moved away, the mirror was blank again. Nothing had been absorbed. And so the anguish would abate—until I saw another billboard, another Italian movie, another waiter, bus-driver, surfer or whatever. In Canberra you might see one such man a fornight. In Paris, on the other hand, there seemed to be at least half a dozen in every carriage on the metro.

I made no serious attempt to assuage the anguish until the marriage broke up, which it did dramatically and painfully at exactly four o'clock one Sunday afternoon. In my experience all life's major tragedies happen on a Sunday afternoon. On this particular Sunday afternoon I was sitting in a hotel room in Wellington, New Zealand, with my back to the room, peacefully writing a letter. It was a beautiful afternoon in late summer, the bay outside was gleaming in the sun and life was full of promise. Elizabeth was there to take up her first diplomatic posting at the High Commission just across the water, it was university vacation and I was spending a week or two with her, helping her settle in, buy a car, find her feet. I had to go back to Canberra the following morning because classes were about to start, but I expected to rejoin her there for longer later in the year. We were a modern couple. Living apart for a few months would be an adventure.

So there we were in the hotel room, with the light from the water dancing on the wall I was facing at my desk and Elizabeth (I thought) reading quietly on the bed behind me. Suddenly the silence was broken with words I'll never forget. 'When you leave tomorrow morning,' Elizabeth said, with the mixture of gentleness and brittleness her family is very good at, 'I don't want you to come back again.' I'd have been less shocked if she'd machine-gunned me.

It took about five years to recover fully from that sentence. It wasn't just the suddenness (although that was brutal), it wasn't just the awfulness of having to go to the airport the next morning and say goodbye forever, which was like dying and made me cringe for months at the mere sound of aircraft engines overhead, it wasn't even just the loss of the sun in the middle of my firmament, which went black and silent and seemed infinitely dead. No, as much as anything it was having to face the fact that I'd failed at being a man. I'd failed humiliatingly for all to see at the single most important task a man has to perform: being married. I'd been taken on approval—not 'for better or for worse, until death do us part', as I had thought—and sent back. Faulty goods. Not sexually faulty so much, actually, in case you're wondering, but not right for a husband. She'd found a better prospect.

At first, not being married was like waking up alone in Bolivia one morning without any Spanish. It wasn't just that I felt unhappy—I felt I did not exist. Once, during a failing attempt to patch things together again in New Zealand, I was driving in deep misery along a country road and suddenly realised that with a jerk of the driving wheel I could crash into something and die. All I had to do was jerk the wheel a fraction to the left or right. I was completely free to do this. So I jerked it and careered into a telegraph pole, snapping it off in the middle and plunging the entire town of Coromandel into darkness. Eventually a jolly policeman arrived, alerted by the power failure. He took one look at the mangled car and one look at me and said: 'Well, you're not a Maori and you're not drunk, so I think we might just forget all about it!' I walked stiffly, brokenly, across the road and caught a bus to the city. I felt cheap.

To piece together a new self I needed a City. In the City you can try on many different masks and no one minds. In the City you're dazzled with choices, you can go mad with them. In the City you can refashion yourself, reclothe yourself, lose yourself and no one's outraged, no one finds you too foul or too askew or even too pure. There everything is permitted. Everything is not permitted in Canberra. When I went to see the bank manager at the university in Canberra to talk about letting my house while I experimented with Sydney, he was outraged. 'Experiment!? Experiment!?' He was seething. 'No, you'll have to sell up if that's what you want to do. Why would you want to experiment?' I muttered something about being a bit bored in Canberra, now I was ... well, *single*, so to speak. 'Bored!' he spat. 'Look, I'm so bored I could chew the leg off this table! But I don't go gallivanting around the country *experimenting*, do I?' I sold the house as quickly as I could, farewelling and thanking every room as I always do when I leave a house (taking what Germaine Greer would call 'spiritual precautions'), and left for Sydney post haste. It was 1978.

Sydney in 1978 seemed to me to be the most voluptuously exciting city on earth. Paris was too stuffy and narcissistic, forever admiring its own reflection, New York was full of feral dangers and people who talked about their mental health *ad nauseam*, Tunis and Tangiers were too penetratingly male, too easy to misread, and all of them, to an Australian (and I know I must be careful how I put this) were strangely provincial. Huge, of course, in the case of Paris and New York, but impenetrably self-absorbed. They thought they were the mothers of civilisation.

Sydney had fewer illusions about itself, was less caught up in its own little rituals of decorum, was more raffish, unpredictable and friendly. It was certainly the best place in Australia to experiment with being what people now called 'gay'. I didn't think of myself as 'gay' when I arrived. I thought of myself as sexually attracted to both women and men—certain women and certain men, although men were certainly more erotically arousing to me. It's hard to explain why. Perhaps, as I can't help suspecting, it's as deeply rooted as genetic makeup, perhaps my brain didn't get the required number of hormone washes (not everyone's does, after all), but I talked to myself about it differently. When I tried to explain it to myself rationally (the Gallic gene in the ascendant), I was inclined to think in terms of (homosexual) men being more excitingly ambiguous, perverse, disruptive of expectations, polymorphous, at least with other men. A man, I found, indeed lots of men, could be John Wayne, Lisa Minnelli, John Travolta and Sandra Dee all in the space of half an hour. Quite a diapason. And if I could learn to loosen up a bit and stop playing a sort of virginal Ben Kingsley every time to all these leads, the combinations could be quite astonishing, although John Wayne was only ever a distant possibility for me, I must admit. There was, too, to be frank, a tendency amongst some Australian males, which I suppose Asian men and women in Australia are only too aware of, to assume that if you were smallish, neatly put together and smooth-skinned, your pleasure must climax in being spreadeagled and impaled, not always deftly. If this tendency asserted itself too abruptly, you had to work quickly to bring out the Sandra Dee dimension in your partner.

All things considered, admitting that there may be many exceptions to the rule, I didn't find that women invited the same diversity of sexual responses. Heterosexual relations appeared to me much more unidirectional in their basic thrust, much less tolerant of a range of sexual personae and much more fixated on the sexual bond. It may appear para-doxical, but for all the emphasis on sexual desirability and indeed on performance in the gay world, in my experience homosexuality actually shifts at least the moral weight off sexual bonding and onto other equally if not more important things. In our kind of basically Christian society, morality is almost a synonym for sexual morality. To be moral means, above all, to be *sexually* moral: that is, to copulate indefinitely with only one person, under contract, a person you have fine feelings for. Such is the moral weight imposed on the sexual bond that in some societies, including supposedly Christian ones, murder is seen as a lesser crime than breaking this sexual bond. Personally, I think slitting one pig's throat is infinitely more immoral than a pleasant evening's copulation with a friend or pick-up. Slitting the pig's throat, however, disrupts no social structures at all, whereas random couplings always have that potential. Gayness, whether it means to or not, undermines this tedious sexual basis to 'morality'. In the end it allows you to concentrate more on what the Church would see as spiritual qualities—selflessness, consideration, affection, friendship, loyalty, constancy, love, intelligence, tolerance, patience—than on sexual bonding. That, at least, has been my experience.

In Sydney in 1978, and for the next four or five years, it was easy for a man or woman wanting to experiment with his or her gayness to do so. Gayness, as I found, is not the same as homosexuality. Tangiers, for example, is stiff with homosexuality—it's offered on the beach, around hotel swimming pools, in the alleys of the casbah, at bus-stations, in cafés and in restaurants. Waiters offer it, streetboys offer it, merchants, guides, bellboys, schoolteachers out for a stroll, half the male population offers it, all you've got to do is stand still for thirty seconds. But Tangiers is completely devoid of gayness, except for the odd watering-place where Europeans gather. Sydney, on the other hand, or at least the Annandale to Bondi belt, was defiantly gay. There were homosexuals dotted about in other parts of the city as well, of course, and homosexual acts, we must presume, were committed all over the place from 1788 onwards (and, needless to say, before 1788, but we're talking about the city). But gayness as such was an inner-city phenomenon, the Annandale to Bondi belt was the hive the bees clustered around, performing their rituals and establishing a culture, which is what gayness is all about. A kind of gay culture, under a different name, had existed in the Eastern suburbs for almost a hundred years, only half-concealed, but by 1978 it was blossoming lushly around Darlinghurst and Paddington. A stroll up Oxford Street in those days revealed a flourishing subculture, not just homosexuals on the prowl. To the out-of-towner it was confrontingly clear that in these seedy, down-at-heel streets and lanes and in the nearby suburbs people were experimenting with a new set of rituals and rites, new value-systems, new readings of history and new political agendas, and they were talking to each other about them in their own newspapers and books and in their own cafés and pubs. Homosexuality was being positively celebrated, as well as practised and theorised about. To a confused young man from Canberra it was a heady experience.

The gay subculture in Sydney also provided a number of examples of that most civilised, most erotically efficient of institutions: the bathhouse. Whereas you might go to a Cairo *hammam* or for that matter to a Moscow *banya* principally to clean out the clogged pores, to take your ease and, of course, to socialise, you would go to a gay bathhouse for all those reasons as well as to divert yourself sexually in a variety of ways. In a highly ritualised way, at the bar, in dimly lit mazes, at the pool table, in the whirlpool—but rarely in the toilets or under the showers, the traditional sites for repressed sexuality to reveal itself—whirlwind courtships (half an hour, five minutes, ten seconds sometimes) were engaged upon, and sometimes consummated, week-long, month-long, even life-long friendships were begun, affairs took wings, fantasies were lived out, desire was given its head. To those outside on the street—perhaps even to those who might sometimes go inside—this was an illicit zone. But once inside you found the 'illicit' had become magically the norm. These clubs did an enormous amount to subvert the preposterous notion that sex must be accompanied by certain sentiments (love, loyalty and so on) in order to be legitimate. As a social control mechanism this notion works reasonably well and quite often in favour of a controlling class which has nothing but disdain for the morality involved, but that's about all that can be said for it, surely. As a character in Dennis Altman's novel *The Comfort of Men* says, 'I've always felt it was fine to be able to separate sex from emotion. The real perversity is to assume the two always go together.'

Still, it was in none of these cabarets, cafés or bathhouses that, in the end, I met Peter. I met train-drivers and professors of philosophy, wheat-farmers, German tourists, jewellers, gardeners, school-teachers, telephonists, actors, doctors, a plethora of solicitors, Maltese migrants, a Chinese financier or two, ballroom-dancing instructors, theological students, at least two Aboriginal activists, painters, no dockers, but social workers, physiotherapists, at least one nationally known RSL official, a pilot or two, dozens of New Zealanders, fathers of four, rabid Christians, car-mechanics—truly a colourful cross-section of the middle and lower classes, people more often than not that I would be unlikely to talk to intimately, let alone become attached to, in any other context. But no one I wanted to link up with indefinitely or who wanted to link up indefinitely with me. It took another quantum leap for that to happen.

It was five o'clock one December afternoon in Paddington and I was at the end of my tether. December is a cruel month for the emotionally insecure. At six o'clock D. was going to drop in—I'd been infatuated with him for a year and a half, our Rorschachs always sliding past each other, gripping just enough to make bliss seem possible, then inching on again—and something told me that today at six, this being December, he would say something to hurry up the process of grinding past each other. I remember sitting upstairs in the stuffy back bedroom of my miniscule Paddington terrace (tourists buses used to stop outside for Japanese tourists to point and laugh and take photographs), gazing out over the swooning city, saying to myself out loud: '*Do* something! *Do* something! Don't just be a chequer on someone else's chequer-board.' Or words to that effect—my psychiatrist had told me to refuse to be a doormat, but I had lots of other metaphors at the ready. I really only had half an hour or so to act on my own advice. The mail was cleared at 5.30 and then and there I decided to place a Personal Advertisement. Ever since *Nation Review* had first startled me with its blunt announcements of sexual availability ('Slim male, forty-two, into raunchy times, dining-out, seeks non-smoking ... ' or 'Well-hung bi guy, clean-shaven, own pad, wants ... No fatties or fems') I'd been aware of this option, but it had seemed dangerous, desperate and doomed to failure. In other words, exciting but vulgar. What would happen if you placed an ad and were then plagued by wizened perverts wanting to tie you up and eat spaghetti out of your armpits? Or, worse, tie you to the bed and then set fire to your house (which happened to a friend of a friend of mine)? Or, if you answered someone else's anonymous ad, what if he turned out to be someone you knew well in an impossibly different capacity? What if, now armed with your telephone number or address, he turned out to be a psychopath or an amiable bore who wouldn't go away? The possibilities for humiliation seemed endless. But I took pen in hand, wrote out a scrupulously honest ad, pretending to be nothing I wasn't and emphasising a liking for a sense of humour, and dashed down to the post with it right on 5.30. I had acted. I had opened up a window in the wall.

The conversation at six did go badly, but in January replies to my ad started to trickle in. One of them *was* from someone I knew, as I discovered on entering the coffee-shop we'd agreed to meet in, one of them was from a tedious Irish comic, but I quickly learnt the drill. *Never* arrange to have dinner—it leaves the evening too open-ended, *always* make a date for lunch or coffee with another appointment looming, *never* expect anything. 'Blessed is he who expecteth little,' as Tom used to say, 'for he generally getteth it.' Then he'd laugh. In fact, I seemed to hit the jackpot. I got a charming, witty letter from a P.T. in Potts Point, he invited me to a tasteful lunch (ratatouille) in one of those huge old terraces in Victoria Street, with views out over the city, the Opera House and the bridge, we decided neither of us was physically *quite* the other's living fantasy and then started slowly to fall in love. With all sorts of things about each other that I suppose neither of us now, after all these years, can imagine living without. Dynamic knitting was the key. After two weeks or so, Peter said in that thought-through, deeply felt but unemotional way he has sometimes: 'If we keep seeing each other, I will fall in love with you and stay with you for good.' This was thrillingly disconcerting. Two weeks became three, three weeks became three months and then three years and now much longer. Marriage seems to me a messy, dishonest arrangement by comparison.

Seven years later, on the balcony at Manly, Yvonne could not have sensed the layers of story—the interweaving sub-plots, the disruptions—behind lunch with her son and his friend in a middle-class suburban house with tasteful wallpaper, a Baluchi on the floor, a Salvatore Zofrea on the wall, Sepik drums on the stairs and a vegetable garden and banana palm out the back. Only when she reads these lines with you will the picture acquire some depth. Not all of it will please or comfort her. It's not the whole truth, of course, but it's one way of trying to tell it.

CHAPTER SIX

Full Circle

'What on earth do you want you bring *that* up for?' grandmother said when eventually, some months after Yvonne and I first met, Yvonne dared mention my name to Mother. 'Have the girls said anything to you? Because if they have I'll really take them to task.' ('The girls', you might remember, must be in their seventies.) In my mind's eye the heavy cedar sideboard is glinting in the half-dark behind them. It was as if Yvonne had been tastelessly harping on the subject for days, but, as you know, she hadn't raised it for nearly half a century. No one had.

One day in the Botanical Gardens, a few months after our first meeting, I'd given Yvonne a few photographs of myself—me as a baby, me at university, me and my wife. Wary of sentiment, I've never been much of a photographer and had little to offer. Yvonne had examined them in silence and taken them home. One of them she chose to put in a small frame and she set this small framed photograph up on the table beside the bed in the room she slept in every other week at Mother's—a small, wordless act of defiance. It was the first morning of a new year, simmering, no doubt, in that steamy concoction of elation, sourness and failed hopes that seeps through the suburbs on New Year's Day. Yvonne took it into her head to point to the photograph and say to her mother: 'Do you know who that is?'

Mother eyed the photograph. Well, it was the elder of Yvonne's two sons, surely. No, it wasn't, Yvonne said. It was someone called Robert. Mother, as I've told you, was not pleased. Nor, I think, was she probably deeply displeased. I imagine she felt curious but riled. One thing was made clear that morning: no word of my existence must be spoken to anyone—not to Yvonne's brothers or sisters or children or anyone else. Mother was very firm about that. As I write the ban has still not been lifted.

We've talked about the ban endlessly, Yvonne and I—in the gardens, where we used to take our sandwiches on sunny days when I was in Sydney, on the telephone, in cafés, on railway stations—but we just go round in circles. I think Yvonne feels she's the rope in a game of tug-of-war between the generations. I want to be named, looked in the eye, told 'Yes, you're part of our story'—not a shameful part, just a part. It's not a matter of blood, it's a matter of storyline. And I want my mother to think of herself as good, seamlessly, uninterruptedly. No one is, I know, but I want her to think of herself like that, for a change. And to begin to do that, she must talk about herself as a whole with those who have known the parts. I don't want to be included in the family Christmas parties, I don't want to follow my half-brothers' children's careers with interest, I don't want to visit my aunts and uncles in hospital when they go in for their operations or even attend my grandmother's funeral—she'd be horrified, I'm sure, to think I might do anything so scandalous. But at those Christmas parties and afternoon teas and family gatherings I'd like to think of my mother sometimes saying, 'I said to Robert last week ... ,' 'Robert and I had a marvellous Indian meal last Saturday, it was ...' and, naturally (who wouldn't?), 'Robert said ...' There's a passage I've always been particularly fond of and amused by in Gogol's comedy *The Government Inspector*. An obsequious provincial nobody called Pyotr Ivanovich Bobchinsky, thinking he's talking to an emissary of the Czar himself (another self-deluded nobody and trickster Khlestakov), says to him in a sudden burst of almost metaphysical desperation: 'If I might humbly beg you, sir, when you get to St Petersburg, please say to all the different big-wigs there—you know, all the senators and admirals—say, "You know, Prince, or Your Excellency, in such-and-such a town lives one Pyotr Ivanovich Bobchinsky." Just say that: "lives one Pyotr Ivanovich Bobchinsky" ... And should you run across the sovereign himself, then say the same thing to the sovereign: "You know, Your Imperial Highness, in such-and-such a town lives one Pyotr Ivanovich Bobchinsky" ... Please excuse me for bothering you with my presence.' He's quickly shown out. I'm not too exercised over the recognition of senators, admirals and sovereigns, but I do understand Bobchinsky's ache to be seen to exist—not approved of, necessarily, or praised, or even loved, but seen to be there. Gogol would have said, I think, that it was a vain desire in every sense, that the only positioning gaze that mattered was God's (I'm paraphrasing), but for most people, with

God's gaze very much a matter of conjecture these days, that's really not by any means enough. A place in the family chronicle would be a good start.

Yvonne is a woman of much grace. I have pondered her grace. As a feminine quality (few men strive for it) it's not in its heyday. It seems too gently contoured, too courteous a quality for our times. Its sense of dignity—unlike refinement, breeding, elegance or mere politeness—seems to come from something too inwardly established, too independent of social forces, class and position to be wholly believed in. Its poise appears too quietist—we crave disruption, disobedience, strength of will, rebellion, we want women to fill the silences with argument and joyful noise and shout over the droning of men. Germaine Greer fits the temper of the times much better, for example, than that irksome figure of fun Mother Teresa, dependent for her goodness on the misery of others. And that's the point, really, I think: grace bears pain and insult, its own and others, and is what it is only in the face of pain and insult. Otherwise it slides into gracefulness and graciousness, mere social accomplishments.

So in the tug-of-war with Mother I do see Yvonne's grace and admire it and falter in any wish to undermine it, while at the same time I ache for her to break through its seal. Your mother's wishes are not sacred, I say to her, her wishes are no more legitimate than yours or mine. Speak to your sons, speak to your sisters—I can speak to anyone about you, but you have to stay silent! She needn't ever know. But Yvonne still says nothing. And the years go by. The moment is never right. 'Yairs,' she says on the telephone, in a Sarsaparilla sort of way, when I urge her to speak, as if she can't say the unsayable, which is that Mother must die first. What is that woman's power?

When Mother went into a Home at long last not so very long ago—she must be nearly one hundred—Yvonne rang me almost feverish with excitement. It was Christmas Day. 'I'm so excited,' she said, 'that I've had to write down what I want to say to you. My mind's in such a whirl I can't trust myself to remember anything.' I felt excited myself. Perhaps now, for the first time since we'd met, now that she no longer had to spend one week out of two looking after her mother and the second week recovering, Yvonne would have time to go shopping in town, go to the cinema, learn Greek as she once said she'd like to, visit her grandchildren, even take a holiday. Perhaps, for the first time in her life, she could catch a plane and visit me in Melbourne.

We'd tried that once before. Choreographing every move minutely, both of us breathless with anticipation, we'd worked out a way for Yvonne to spend most of one of her free weeks with me in Melbourne. For the first time we'd have breakfast, lunch and dinner together, say goodnight and good morning, talk about nothing in particular, go shopping together, even sit and stare into the distance together—all the sorts of things mothers and sons do together hundreds of times over the years. Yvonne had no dentist's appointment, no doctor's appointment, Mother was not sickening for anything—the coast was clear. I even went to

Sydney the day before so that we could fly to Melbourne
together; I didn't want her first trip in a plane to be an
ordeal, I wanted every minute of that week to be a kind of special gift.

I was staying the night with an old friend in Darlinghurst and
had given Yvonne the number, just in case she needed a few
words of reassurance. At about five o'clock in the afternoon the
telephone rang and I heard her familiar voice saying in the
slightly self-deprecating way she has: 'Hullo, is that you,
Robert?'

'Yes,' I said brightly, thinking we'd be checking again
whether one sweater was enough for Melbourne in February or
whether just in case she should bring two.

'How are you?' she said, politely, sounding awfully faint.

'I'm fine. How are you?'

'Well, I'm not too good, Robert.'

'Oh, dear,' I said, slightly irritated (to be perfectly honest), but
steeling myself to be firm that she must come, sniffles or no sniffles. 'What's wrong?'

Her son was dead. He had died in horribly distressing circumstances. She'd only known for an hour. She was very
apologetic about any bother she was causing. The next day
she did indeed leave Sydney on the longest trip she'd ever
made, to the property her son had had on the coast several
hundred kilometres to the north, for his funeral. By the time she
got back from the funeral it was her week on at Mother's
again and, as luck would have it, Mother was in a particularly
demanding mood that week, too.

Later, thinking it was only practical, Yvonne asked her doctor for a certificate to say she hadn't been able to travel. After all, it seemed a shame to make a gift of the fare to the insurance company. Her doctor said he couldn't do that because he had no evidence that her son had died or that she'd been unfit to travel. Even Yvonne found his attitude a little unreasonable, but she let the matter drop.

A year later, with Mother now in a Home, I thought we'd try again. Again the coast seemed clear: no medical check-ups, no family birthday parties, no advanced pregnancies, no blocked nasal passages, even Mother was being not unduly uncooperative, if a trifle tetchy at losing her fiefdom. I rang a few days before to tell Yvonne I'd bought two tickets to *Phantom of · the Opera*, just to apply a little moral pressure in case she wavered for some reason or other at the last minute. No, no, she was excited about it, she was half-packed already, she was not a bit nervous about flying for the first time alone, she was booking a cab for 9.30 … The evening before she was to come I was actually ironing her pillowcases for her when the telephone went. Unfortunately Mother had taken a turn for the worse. Mother could die. Even if she had a peaceful night and started to improve, Yvonne could not possibly leave her, she'd only be on tenterhooks the whole time if she came, she wouldn't enjoy it, it was out of the question. I could barely speak with … well, it was a kind of grief. But could say nothing. Not a syllable that wasn't sympathetic and understanding. I went to *Phantom of the Opera* and loathed every note. By then grandmama had recovered remarkably and, though frail, she continues to enjoy oustandingly good health and presence of mind for one of such advanced years. She asks after me fondly and seems genuinely pleased that Yvonne and I have the contact we have. Despite having spent years of her life in her domestic service (only she and one brother have in effect no spouse—the other five brothers and sisters, having spouses and families, have been excused from anything more onerous than flying visits) Yvonne has nothing but the deepest love for her mother, laughing about her tyrannical ways as if they were nothing more than colourful and expressing the view from time to time, almost as if to caution me against jumping to conclusions, that her mother is by any account a very good person.

We often find ourselves using words differently, Yvonne and I. In most families I expect you start to use them differently rather gradually, and argue about them until you reach some sort of agreement not to argue about them any further. Is that how it happens? In our case it's been all much more sudden. And so when Yvonne speaks of one or other of her relatives, a man I might think of as narrow-minded and hopelessly mired in oppressive moral codes, and describes him as 'highly moral', 'principled' and 'good', I'm at a loss as to what to say. Who am I to say anything? It's none of my business. We use words like 'moral', 'principled' and 'good' very differently, for legitimate, socially determined reasons. Her surviving son, she seems to think, might use such words more the way I do. All the same, there have been occasions when I've found the family's 'goodness' an affront.

There are some things it's so hard to find the words for or

the courage to say that we say nothing. And of those things the
hardest of all—even as I write I'm aware I've never put it into
words before—is ... and here I feel an abstract noun or two
begging to be used: 'guilt', is it? or 'the moral burden of
good fortune'? What I need, I think, is not a noun, but
some form of speech that's more discursive. In telling each
other our stories, we started out by calling to each other in
short strings of words across a gap. We mined for the words as
if our lives were dictionaries. We recounted lives which, led
though they were not far from each other in terms of miles
(across a river once, in that beachside town, in Sydney),
were led in other ways within completely different worlds. In
neither world was there ever much money, yet I feel in the
world I grew up in there was a *plenty* and a freedom I can't
regret I had. I'm torn, you see, between regret I can scarcely
measure for what happened to Yvonne and no regret at all that
my life took the course it did. In some deep place Yvonne is
probably torn in a similar way, even more painfully. So
when the time comes to say some of these things out loud, I
feel the air becoming fraught with emotions, passions,
words—whole skeins of unspoken words—to do with loss,
with thwarting, with guilty debt, with wrongs never to be
righted, with terrible *if only's* and clouded questions about fate.
We back away then—or, at least, I do, being in truth the
guiltier party—and exchange more stories.

❖ ❖ ❖

Speaking of stories, the French business Yvonne alluded to in our first conversation intrigued me and I determined to get to the bottom of it. One way or another it had hung about me all my life. Sometimes I'd rather clung to it in the hope it might explain some of my evident peculiarities, certain singular ways of behaving and speaking. And Frenchness was not only rare in Australia but also vaguely chic, in a way being Bulgarian or Finnish could never be.

The whole thing fell apart last year in a library in Riom. Well, not the *whole* thing, but the central storyline. It happened very suddenly, as a matter of fact. You've probably never heard of Riom and may never hear of it again. It's provincial France at its most charmingly leaden. Still, you never know, it produced the Desaix clan (with one 's') and in their own way, as I've hinted, they were once quite illustrious. Family seats and so forth.

Riom is completely round and sits on a small hill near Vichy in Auvergne, a placid part of central France where in spring, according to my guidebook, the stables fill with lowing, the dovecotes with cooing and the peasants were traditionally noted for their sobriety. As a result of this sobriety no local cuisine ever developed—the guide-book is categorical about this: *il n'en est rien*—and the main traditional dish is a cabbage and lard *potée*, whose characteristic aroma is said to be unforgettable. On the other hand Riom has a saint, the fifth-century St-Amable, *dont la tradition rapporte bon nombre de miracles*, the fourteenth-century Duke Jean de Berry favoured Riom above all the other residences in his

Duchy, and a hair from the head of St Joan (now permanently misplaced) was once kept at the Town Hall.

I arrived at Riom one soft October afternoon intent on fleshing out my ancient roots. I took a room at the Hôtel Desaix on the boulevard Desaix only a hop, step and a jump from the Fontaine Desaix along the boulevard to the right and the restaurant Desaix along the boulevard to the left. It was all very affirming. Even the *patronne* of the hotel reminded me strikingly of my mother Yvonne: small-boned, almost frail, marooned somehow, but spirited, refusing to surrender. They could have been sisters.

Before setting out for the gorges of the Sioule River to the west to look for the villages my ancestors lived in—men like Guillaume des Aix, for example in 1287, Pierre des Haies in 1335, Jehan des Saix in 1401, Jean lez Aix a little later, not to mention the illustrious Louis des Aix Veygoux, as he styled himself, the just sultan of Upper Egypt, the only member of his family to espouse the Revolution—I decided to stroll around the darkening town to see if any spirits cried out to me from the stones. Up the narrow, shabby streets I went, the gathering gloom punctuated the way it is in Europe by brilliant squares of light: chocolate shops, charcuteries, shoe shops, *salons de thé*. At the top of the hill near the clock-tower I came at last to the real Hôtel Desaix, the family's *hôtel particulier* or town residence with its walled garden and archway and heavy iron gates. No spirits cried out from the blackened stones. It appeared to have been turned into a museum and art gallery. There was a poster on the gate advertising an exhibition of Zulu art by Ousmane Sow, who as far as I could make out wasn't even a Zulu. I remember feeling very faintly affronted.

Out to the west, out towards the meandering Sioule— you could see them clearly at the foot of the hill—stretched pale fields of rye and buckwheat, apple orchards and clumps of ash. Out there somewhere, waiting for me, stood the ruins of the family château of St-Hilaire d'Ayat with its stone wells and mouldering seigneurial dovecotes. Above some doorway somewhere you could still see the family coat-of-arms, apparently, engraved in the stone: a line of golden cockleshells. Half in a trance I started wandering down the hill towards my own Hôtel Desaix.

After a moment or two I found myself passing the Municipal Library of Riom. It was a 'welcoming space', according to the notice on the door, 'but also lively'. I was intrigued by the word *but* and decided to go in. What the notice meant was that anyone could go in but, like municipal libraries everywhere, it was basically an adventure playground for infants and a safe haven for teenage courting couples. I took a seat in the Reference Section and started perusing slim volumes on the Desaix family. They were crammed full of wonderful names like Marie-Anne-Adélaïde Farjon des Charmes and El Kab des Mamelouks. Then all of a sudden, at the back of an unpromising self-published tract, I chanced upon a family tree. I gasped with excitement and all the other readers glanced up. I started to unfold it with a kind of numb awe. There at the very top was

Aubert des Ayes (1287), branching out into dozens of Gilbertes and Gaspards and Annes and Antoines and Jacques and Yvonnes and Etiennes ... but how to make sense of the multitude of little paired boxes at the bottom of the tree? My eyes were racing up and down branches and twigs and tiny twiglets ... *célibataire, sans issue* ... and there, suddenly, with awful clarity, I came at last to Léon Joseph Aymard Desaix: hunter of small game, active in the Resistance, died in his bed 3rd November 1941 a bachelor and ... *avec ce personnage haut en couleur ... with this highly colourful personality ... s'éteignit le nom de Desaix. ... the name of Desaix was extinguished.* Extinguished? I was thunder-struck. But it was *my* name and, apart from anything else, there was one in the Clermont-Ferrand telephone-book, purportedly living not ten miles from where I sat. Of course, peering stunned at the ceiling, I soon understood that what the architect of this withered family tree meant was that *those* Desaixs existed no longer, the Desaixs of châteaux and campaigns against the Mamelouks. The only Desaixs of any account, the only Desaixs one would be interested in claiming any connection with, had died out years ago in a flurry of *célibataires* and childless couples.

I gathered my wits and stood up from the table, almost expecting the other readers to point at me and snigger, whispering 'Fraud!'. I turned and faced the bookshelf behind me. There, not two inches from my nose, was the *Grande encyclopédie biographique* in twenty volumes. I took down Volume Six and turned to Dessaix with *two* s's. And there, like some instruction from a patrimonial guardian angel, was an entry on *another* General Dessaix, also a Napoleonic general, veteran of the Russian campaign (how appropriate), wounded near Moscow ... I could hardly believe my eyes. It was all so simple. There'd been a mistake. The s's had confused people. It was a pity about Egypt, but Russia had possibilities, there were certain synchronicities ...

Back I went to the Hôtel Desaix and packed for Paris. What a displeasing little *bourg* Riom had turned out to be, squatting on its plain of rye with its bogus saints and cabbage-and-lard hotpot and dead-end *petite noblesse*. General Dessaix with two s's hailed from Savoy. I rather liked the sound of that. The moment I got to Paris I found a little restaurant called 'Le Savoyard' in a backstreet off the boulevard de Sébastopol and settled in there for the evening to think myself into a different storyline altogether, something much more alpine, icier, more severe, hard-edged—loftier, in a word. Now I came to think about it there in 'Le Savoyard' (although the *patronne* didn't look at all like my mother), I'd always felt a certain ... how should I put it? *affinity* for that part of France, I even rather liked Geneva, which everyone else found so cold and alien. General Joseph-Marie Dessaix was looking very promising indeed.

So, forgetting Cairo and the Mamelukes and the fatal ball at the battle of Marengo, I began my investigations into my Savoyard with eagerness: Joseph-Marie Dessaix, *général de division, comte de l'Empire*—a count, one could do worse—a man possessed, it transpired, of a rude *indépendence de caractère* which dissuaded Napoleon from making him a Marshal. Preferring honour to 'enriching himself at the expense of others' he apparently died poor. My principled uncles would no doubt find that admirable. He was wounded in the battle for Moscow, made governor of Berlin, and had a number of children and nephews who were not at all *célibataires* or childless. I very much liked the sound of Count Joseph-Marie of the Thonon-les-Bains branch of the family on Lake Geneva. All that military *éclat* was a little off-putting, but there were compensations: the Russian connection, the sense of good family and honourable service, and even certain literary pretensions. At about the turn of the nineteenth century his father, for instance, Charles Eugène Joseph, wrote the following nobly instructive poem:

PRIDE IN BIRTH
For my Grandchildren

Behold the vainglorious braggart, infatuated with his breeding,
Boasting at every turn about his ancestors and forebears,
Feeding his pride on marvellous deeds (not his, but theirs),
Of calls to follow in their footsteps, though, unheeding!

Instead of blushing at the emptiness of futile titles,
He grasps at some importance for himself in trivialities,
And tries to expiate, through others' virtues (not his own),
The error of his birth and blundering fate's banalities!

A Mother's Disgrace

Blind in its choices, whether at Thonon-les-Bains or Rome,
Making now a palace, now a simple thatched hut home,
In an instant birth can make of the obscurest embryo a count or earl,
While greatness in a man can take a patient century to unfurl.

Leaving as you must your cradles, my dear children,
Fear the lying bait of valorous titles, shun delusion;
Aspire to virtue, pity wickedness and all its wiles:
Good will then be safely yours—all else is vain illusion.

Well put, although the stench of piety is perhaps a little
strong for modern tastes. But Charles Eugène Joseph's heart
was in the right place, surely. (And you have to remember that,
blithely unaware of all those robust Germanic roots in English,
the French don't mean to sound as pompous with their
Latin abstractions as they do.) Be that as it may, the 'lying bait
of valorous titles' still has some allure in suburban Sydney, I
suspect. To be completely frank, I can't deny it still has
some allure for me. But I can agree it's 'vain illusion'. In
fact, I think now the Savoyard General and his sons and
nephews are just a tale that's told. I've scrabbled around in
their twisted family trees—all those Eugènes, Jean-
François-Aimés, Jean-Marie-Josephs, Constances and
Joséphines, all those *capitaines* and *commandants*, *sergents* and
magistrats, all those *mortes sans enfants* and *mortes jeunes*—and
really, I see no evidence they have anything to do with us whatever. Why do we insist on walking backwards towards our
deaths with our eyes fixed stupidly on past chimeras?

Full Circle

Because, I suppose, we find our utter ordinariness, our run-of-the-millness, not even to speak of our cosmic insignificance, utterly intolerable. 'Good stock'! Good grief, it's brambles and mud as far as the eye can see.

It's true that in the valleys of the Haute-Savoie, hardly half an hour's drive from Geneva's cold heart, around the villages of Marignier and Faucigny and the forest of St Jeoire, there were families called Dessaix. Tax records from 1464 make mention of the *domus nobilis Amedei de Saxo* (from the Latin *saxum*, stone) and the *domus nobilis* branched and split and spread into Dessaix, Dussaix, de Saix, some doubtless less *nobiles* than others. And in the middle of the nineteenth century, as I now know, the Haute-Savoie was prey to numerous so-called emigration agencies, shipping Savoyards (few dukes or counts, though, naturally) to North Africa, America and Argentina. According to one account, 'our valleys rang with the call to emigrate', they were littered with 'posters, prospectuses and brochures' and aswarm with the unscrupulous agents of governments anxious to populate their 'pampas and desert prairies' with the scrapings from Savoyard villages. Just a scratch at the bottom of the papers they waved would open the gates of paradise. I think my great-great-grandfather Peter or his father, impoverished carpenters or wheelwrights, probably signed up in the mid-1850s, got stuck in Ireland on the way to the New World and ended up in St Leonards in Sydney, not far from where I lived and went to school—still wheelwrights, still poor, still nobody. I think what I am is a small, tied-off bastard

185

nodule at the end of a twig on a stick-thin branch of the utterly commonplace bush they planted here.

Not in my head, though. There Amadeus de Saxo and his *domus nobilis*, the quilted valleys of the Arve and the Giffre (brilliant, paint-box green on my map of Rhône-Alpes), the long, tangled lines of Savoyard families of doctors and poets and heroes of the Russian campaign lie like a homeland I had strangely misplaced—I admit it. My fierce sense of being self-made, 'as if I'd thought myself up', as the Russians say, is largely shattered. I'd have liked to think I'd woven myself cunningly out of an assortment of odd threads and yarn, chosen with taste and freely, but from the moment I met Yvonne in that house in Longueville I've doubted that's really what I've done.

Forgetting freedom for a moment, even the fashionable notion of a self as the unique point at which various discourses intersect (discourses about family, God, class, intelligence, taste, sexuality—they're almost infinite) doesn't seem adequate to describe what I now see. What I now see is something much more old-fashioned, much closer to common wisdom: looking for the first time across the dining-room table at my grandmother, soft-skinned and haughty, watching the way she spoke and smiled, the way she took control of the room around her, the way my mother mixed diplomacy and self-assertion, charging the air around her with unspoken retorts —sitting looking at all this I had to think of blood. I'm no geneticist and will stick with a simpler concept. Discourses may intersect as they will and the self may kaleidoscope into thousands of unique patterns over the years, but some things are surely given. To live dynamically (as it seems to me now) the important thing is not so much to deny what is given but to confront it constantly, to prick it, mock it and outrage it with what is not.

I once met an Abkhazian novelist (I mention this in the spirit of pricking) called Fazil Iskander, a Gogolian-Marquezian writer from Sukhumi on the Black Sea. He's been to Australia, but I first met him in his Moscow flat in one of those apartment blocks on Red Army Street reserved, in Soviet times at least, for writers. Over tea the talk veered round to religion. Abkhazia is partly Christian, partly Muslim, although the dominant ideology was in those days atheist. So the topic was bound to come up. I asked Fazil if he was Christian or Muslim. 'Oh, I'm a non-believer,' he said, using a much less strident word than 'atheist' with its overtones of Soviet dogmatism. 'But I don't want to rid the world of believers. There will always be believers and there will always be non-believers. I like it like that. I'd hate to live in a world where there were no believers.' In saying that, hardly noticing he'd said it, he'd inadvertently prised open some fuggy, boxed-in part of my brain. (It's funny the way that can happen: people can throw you a word or two over a shoulder on the way to catch a bus and completely alter the way you think about everything.) Sitting right there on his sofa, staring at the blue-and-gold teapot, I thought seriously for the first time of letting the believer inside myself talk to the non-believer, letting the knowing part converse in good humour with the mystified and the credulous with the sceptical. It was a wicked feeling.

As I've told you, in my childhood the bush and brambles with their spiders and snakes and blue-tongued lizards always belonged firmly down the back. In summer the faintest smell of fire sent Jean and Tom out into the backyard to peer through the trees into the gully. The street, on the other hand, was kerbed, the front lawn clipped and there was a proper geometry to the front garden. The backyard and the frontyard met at the trellis at the side of the house: viciously beautiful climbing roses facing the street, the back a warm jungle of honeysuckle, never trimmed and rustling and creaking with small animals and insects dealing death to each other. There was, you see, in that child's proto-type of paradise a clear division. It's taken years to start to break that down.

And so, in that new prickly spirit, still circling around the question of who we are at any moment, I'd like to broach a subject which will almost certainly strike you as bizarre. After all, everyone is so knowledgeable nowadays, everyone seems to *know* everything about everything, about wave particles, synapses, probability theory, black holes, Wittgenstein, there's no need any more merely to *believe* in any-thing. What I want to say is bound up with coincidence. Perhaps there's a better word ('irony of circumstance', 'random synchronicity') but 'coincidence' will do for now. Life is littered with coincidences, of course. This narrative is lit-tered with coincidences, for that matter, as characters in my tale brush past each other unaware that from the point of view of a storyteller yet to emerge narrative lines are mysteriously knotting, branching and forming patterns.

Some of the litter is probably just that. I type the almost never met-with word 'Auvergne', for example, stop typing, go out to the mail-box and take out a colourful card from Carmel Bird emblazoned with the words 'Aux Fruits Glacés d'Auvergne'. I'm in a plane reading Mark Henshaw's novel *Out of the Line of Fire*, I come to the word 'Klagenfurt' and as I say it softly to myself the pilot's voice comes through my headphones saying: 'We're now flying over Klagenfurt.' You smile at such coincidences, such minor synchronicities, but put them down quite reasonably to random intersections of trajectories, you don't ask yourself as a rule if God means you to go to Klagenfurt or buy a box of glazed fruit. They might ask themselves that sort of fatuous question in cultures where it's not understood yet that the universe is just a lot of particles flying apart and then collapsing back again, but not here, not the sort of people we know.

But (and this is the really awkward part) some coincidences have appeared to me not to be random. Or to have, like wave particles, a patterned randomness. To believe them simply random would, ironically, be to strain credulity. What, then, are they? All I can do is explain how I perceive them, even if you're inclined to relegate them instantly to the glazed fruit category. If you stand on a hill watching a train wind its way along a railway-track below on your right, the fact that it's derailed by the stalled car at the crossing further along the track on your left does not appear random to you. That's not a word that would adequately describe what you see happen. To the car's doomed driver there might appear to be a randomness to what happens—the car stalls at the random confluence of millions of trajectories: faulty carburettor, his mother's meeting with his father, the train-driver's migraine—and the train's driver and passengers might well agree with him as they career off the rails and capsize. But to me, up on the hill, the coincidence of the train and the car is not so much foreordained, or even predictable (how am I to know? perhaps the car will buck abruptly into life and off the tracks) as *in the order of things*, from a certain point of view. Once I'm up on the hill.

Sometimes I've had a sense of seeing things simultaneously both from the driver's point of view and the observer's at the top of the hill. It doesn't feel strange or luminous; on the contrary, it feels decidedly ordinary and right. Sometimes the simultaneity occurs in your head before it does in the world, so to speak, which feels a little odder. Sometimes you feel empowered to make an actuality of a possibility common sense tells you has a billion-to-one chance of coming true. I know we're told by the ultra-sane that perception is a brain function, a matter of electricity, atoms, nerves and so forth, but that doesn't quite accord with my experience. It's rather embarrassing to have to say so, but it doesn't.

I'm standing in the main street of Rabat in Morocco. It's quite a large town, almost half a million people live here. I've just arrived to visit a friend called Ahmed H. I have his address and I know it's right because I've written to him there and had several replies. But when I show it to taxi-drivers they shake their heads and tell me it makes no sense to them. I go back into the airline office I've just emerged from to see if anyone there can decipher it for me. I draw a complete blank. Outside in the glare of the sun I can see the street seething with people. I've been flying since yesterday and feel desperate to arrive and sink into a long sleep. I sit down in the anonymous cool of the office and withdraw, upwards. (You're smirking, I can tell, but don't smirk too soon.) I can't actually *see* anything yet from where I am, but I'm up there. Now comes the tricky part. The seething street does not become *unreal* to me exactly, it becomes in the blink of an eye more what I'd call *relatively* real, and what I have to do is to hook it up to a different relative reality, hovering above it. There's a meshing in the offing, I can feel it in my bones. (I don't apologise for this, it happened as surely as you picked up this book—I've just reread my letter home describing it to Jean and Tom.) And so I walk out into the street and head off ... I'd have to say 'at random' on the level of the street, but in no direction at all on the other circular, stationary level above. And so I walk in the street and stay stock-still in my mind. Then I cast down my hook. I stop a man and say to him: 'Do you know this street?' 'Yes, of course, I know it,' he says, 'and I know that house because Ahmed is my nephew. I'll take you there now.' And he does. And as we walk and I let myself down into the street again, it almost scoots away from under me when I hit it.

And now I'm in Caracas with my wife. Again, we've just arrived. We have virtually no money at all, just the odd centivo: no one will change our Austrian schillings into bolivars and there's no letter for me at the American Express office to tell me where the money I'm expecting has been sent. All we've got to eat is crackers and cheese saved from the plane. It's time for radical action. Out into the street I go, drifting upwards. Venezuelan streets claim a lot of your attention, frankly, but something in me is edging upwards towards stillness. I come to a bus-stop. A bus draws up and I get on it. I'm so stationary and circular inside now I'm only very faintly aware of the need to cast my hook, but I cast it and draw the street up towards me. I get off the bus and walk straight into the Royal Bank of Canada. I've never heard of the Royal Bank of Canada and, on the level of the street (so to speak), have no reason to be there. I approach a teller and and he hands me my cash. Again, I'm not exactly surprised, but deeply satisfied. Before I have time to let the world scoot off with me again, a woman comes up to me, right there inside the bank. 'Excuse me,' she says, as matter-of-factly as if she were about to ask me the time, 'I thought you might like to read this.' And she hands me an article cut from a newspaper, in English, explaining in detail the precise ... what shall we call it? the newspaper called it a spiritual process, but that's such a messy word ... let's just say the precise metaphysical and indeed religious experience I have just been through, in words and phrases I'd made mine years ago. This does startle and move me. But the woman has gone. You don't expect this sort of thing in Venezuela.

Now, I'm not an other-worldly sort of person, nor a particularly irrational one. I actually make a very bad mystic. Indeed, any adept of Jung would pick me immediately, I'm sure, as locked far too firmly into reasoning and analysis at the expense of the psyche's more elemental and free-wheeling possibilities. So why am I sharing thoughts with you which must seem to you as silly as crystals? Why invite your scorn? Because I'd like to make it clear for the record that, as I see it now, 'random' is an inadequate description of the course my life has taken—as poor as 'self-determined' or 'genetically determined'. Not that I want to suggest by that that I think any God in any orthodox religious sense has had anything at all to do with anything, or that I think some things are 'meant to be' (by whom, exactly?), but by the same token it's hard for me to reconcile my experience with the idea that all reality is just the aftermath of a mindless big bang. I feel, in other words, a great wheeling-about inside since that first night in Cairo. I feel I can see what a friend of mine, a Russian and a non-believer, means when he says: 'Why must God be a noun? It's a verb!' Perhaps it's just a case of overactive quantum particles in my synapses—they really do appear to have a mind of their own sometimes, those things.

❖ ❖ ❖

There's no operatic ending to this tale, I'm afraid. In fact, to be perfectly frank, it isn't the sort of tale that has an ending. I did give it a beginning, I admit, but just for purposes of seduction. I could write you an ending, if you insist:

Late the following summer, surrounded by her seven children and secure in their love, Grandmother passed peacefully away. Released now from the rôle of dutiful daughter, Yvonne began slowly to live life as she wanted— to speak of her life as a good life in all its parts, to enjoy its graces, to travel a little, to spend time with her children as the mood took her, even to learn Greek at last, just for fun ...

No, that won't really do. It's insipid and graceless. What about something like this:

At long last the day arrived. In a turmoil of contradictory emotions I sped along the freeway towards Melbourne airport, scanning the sky for signs of her plane swooping in to land. Not five minutes from now, not four not three ...

But no, that really won't do either. It does sound a bit like me, I agree, but you can tell my heart's not quite in it. The last thing that happened, if that's what you mean by an ending is this:

Last Sunday evening, as I do every second Sunday, according to our secret tradition, I dialled Yvonne's number and waited for her voice to interrupt the burring. 'Oh, Robert!' she'd say any second now—she always does and I get a bolt of pleasure—'I was just about to turn you on on the radio!' (Oh dear, I always think, I hope I haven't got anyone saying ... well, 'fuck' or anything on the show tonight ... or a lesbian separatist or ...)

But that will hardly satisfy you, either, if you really crave an ending. If you really crave straight lines. I told you: this is a tale without an ending. I have told you the truth. Now trust me.

Inside Outside

ANDREW RIEMER

ON A FREEZING NOVEMBER DAY IN 1946, ANDREW Riemer, then a ten-year-old with mumps, left a bomb-scarred Budapest on his way to Australia. A few days before Christmas in 1990 he returned to the city of his birth where, amid the decay of a world waking from totalitarian rule, he tried to reconstruct the past from shreds of memory and family myth.

In the years between, his career had taken him from being an expert in French-knitting, a skill acquired when, unable to speak English, he was put in a class for intellectually handicapped children, to Sydney University, where he now teaches English Literature.

Andrew Riemer has written a classic. Witty, lucid, heartrending and wonderfully funny. No reader will ever forget his two worlds, or the profound questions he asks about them.
JILL KER CONWAY

Travelling Light

ROBYN DAVIDSON

*It's been a long time since I claimed some solitude in this blessed
landscape; since I've done without life's little props. Here I have no
friend, no dog, no radio, no clock, no phone, no roof, no body
pollutants. The clackety-clack of the typewriter travels out into the
valley and gets lost in expanses of forest and paperbark swamp. I'm
the only one around.*

For ten years Robyn Davidson has been travelling light. Across
the desert, across America on a Harley-Davidson, or walking
through the bush of ghosts by night. In these articles that
make up *Travelling Light*, the bestselling author of *Tracks* takes
us into wilds of many countries — as well as countries of the
mind.

A born writer
DAILY TELEGRAPH

A perceptive and sensitive observer.
SYDNEY MORNING HERALD

Wild Cat Falling

MUDROOROO

*W*ild *Cat Falling* is the story of an Aboriginal youth, a 'bodgie' of the early sixties, who grows up on the ragged outskirts of a country town, falls into petty crime, goes to gaol, and comes out to do battle once more with the society that put him there. Its publication in 1965 marked a unique literary event, for this was the first novel by any writer of Aboriginal blood to be published in Australia. As well, it is a remarkable piece of literature in its own right, expressing the dilemmas and conflicts of the young Aborigine in modern Australian society with memorable insight and stylishness.

'A friend always leaves a track —
this is the teaching of the Aborigines.'
DAVID UNAIPON

'It was in 1965 that Mudrooroo put down tracks in this, the first novel by an Aboriginal Australian. Writing can be a generous and friendly gesture, (because it makes communication an instructive pleasure) but for Mudrooroo it was also a struggle, just to get his book out. His tracks are still here, for you to follow them up and to see which way he was going then, or even which way Australia was going then, especially in terms of its treatment of the Aboriginal peoples.'
STEPHEN MUECKE, *from the Introduction*

I have a feeling it doesn't really matter what
other films I make, I'll always be introduced as
Bruce Beresford who made Breaker Morant

Bruce Beresford

PETER COLEMAN

Bruce Beresford makes powerful movies, ones from the heart. The apparent ease of his finished films perhaps denied him an Oscar for *Driving Miss Daisy*, 'the film that directed itself'. In this first critical study of Beresford's work, Peter Coleman takes us on location with the director on his latest movie *Rich in Love*, and through extensive interviews we go behind the scenes of the making of all his films.

Here is the director at work — the strict storyboarding of every scene; the shifting sands of epic productions like *King David*; the earliest, witty experimental shorts and his feeling for great stories of our times; *Tender Mercies*, *The Getting of Wisdom*, *Crimes of the Heart* and *Black Robe*. Peter Coleman has combined his knowledge of the developing Australian film industry with his long-standing friendship with Beresford so the reader can glimpse the trials and tribulations of Australia's most self-critical film director.

Robert Dessaix is a well-known broadcaster, critic and translator. He studied at Moscow University in the late sixties and early seventies and for almost twenty years taught Russian language and literature at the Australian National University and University of New South Wales. Since 1985 he has been the producer and presenter of the weekly ABC Radio program 'Books and Writing' and has published a number of short stories, critical essays and translations of Russian writers such as Chekhov, Dostoyevsky and Turgenev. He recently edited the Oxford University Press anthology *Australian Gay and Lesbian Writing*.